*Approach love and cooking
with reckless abandon.*

The Dalai Lama

Other books by Merlinda Bobis

Pag-uli, Pag-uwi, Homecoming (poetry)

White Turtle / The Kissing (short fiction)

Summer Was a Fast Train Without Terminals (poetry)

Cantata of the Warrior Woman Daragang Magayon (poetry)

Ang Lipad ay Awit sa Apat na Hangin / Flight Is Song on Four Winds (poetry)

Rituals (poetry)

and coming soon:

The Solemn Lantern Maker

Banana Heart Summer

a novel by Merlinda Bobis

Delta
Trade Paperbacks

BANANA HEART SUMMER
A Delta Book

PUBLISHING HISTORY
Murdoch Books Australia hardcover edition published 2005
Delta trade paperback edition / June 2008

Published by
Bantam Dell
A Division of Random House, Inc.
New York, New York

Library of Congress Catalog Card Number: 2008000768

Delta is a registered trademark of Random House, Inc., and the colophon is a
trademark of Random House, Inc.

ISBN 978-0-385-34112-7

Printed in the United States of America
Published simultaneously in Canada

www.bantamdell.com

BVG   10 9 8 7 6 5 4 3 2 1

ACKNOWLEDGMENTS

Thanks to Jacqueline Lo, who read with the heart of the palate
to Margaret Gee, who affirmed the taste of a banana heart summer
to Reinis Kalnins, who lured me into the flavors of daily miracles
to Anna Rogers, my gracious editor, and to Juliet Rogers, Kay Scarlett, Diana Hill, Tracy Loughlin and all the believers of Murdoch Books who crafted a "little gem"
to my family and first home, their tender constancy
to all who appease our hungers

and to the mothers and daughters who taught me
that love is prickly sweet on the tongue.

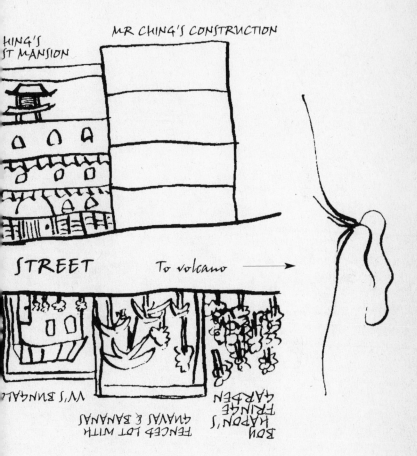

HING'S
ST MANSION

MR CHING'S CONSTRUCTION

STREET

To volcano →

VV'S BUNGALOW

FENCED LOT WITH
GUAVAS & BANANAS

BON
HADON'S
FRINGE
GARDEN

CONTENTS

the heart of
the matter

For those who love to love and eat
For those who long to love and eat

When we laid my baby sister in a shoebox, when all the banana hearts in our street were stolen, when Tiyo Anding stepped out of a window perhaps to fly, when I saw guavas peeking from Manolito's shorts and felt I'd die of shame, when Roy Orbison went as crazy as Patsy Cline and lovers eloped, sparking a scandal so fiery that even the volcano erupted and, as a consequence, my siblings tasted their first American corned beef, then Mother looked at me again, that was the summer I ate the heart of the matter.

So how did it all begin?

With this lesson about the banana heart from Nana Dora, the chef of all the sweet snacks that flavored our street every afternoon, except Sundays.

"Close to midnight, when the heart bows from its stem, wait for its first dew. It will drop like a gem. Catch it with your tongue. When you eat the heart of the matter, you'll never grow hungry again."

From the site of her remark, I will take you through a tour of our street and I will tell you its stories. Ay, my street of wishful sweets and spices. All those wishes to appease stomachs and make hearts fat with pleasure. And perhaps sweeten tempers or even spice up a storyteller's tongue.

Let's begin with appeasement, my first serious business venture long ago. Let's begin with a makeshift kitchen, a hut with no walls, under banana trees in bloom. Here, Nana Dora parked her fragrant wok at two in the afternoon. By three, the hungry queue began.

two

Turon: the melody

The sound of deep frying was a delectable melody. Instantly loud and aggressive when the *turon* hit the pool of boiling coconut oil, then pulling back. The percussion was inspired to be subtle.

"Ay, it sounds and smells like happiness," I said, nose and ears as primed as my sweetened tongue. Happiness that is not subtle at all, I could have added. Such is the fact about the *turon,* which is half a slice of sugar banana and a strip of jackfruit rolled in paper-thin rice wrapping, then dusted with palm sugar and fried to a crisp brown. How could such fragrance be subtle? My nose twitched, my mouth watered, my stomach said, buy, buy.

"So you're an expert on happiness?" Nana Dora asked. Her face glowed with more than sweat and the fire from her stove.

"Believe me, your cooking is music, Nana Dora."

"Hoy, don't flatter me, Nenita." She made a face. But I could see the flush deepening on her cheeks, the hand patting wisps of hair in place and the coy turning of the neck, as if a lover had just whispered sweet nothings to her ear.

I hovered closer, bent towards the wok, no, bowed, paying

obeisance to its melody: mi-fa-so-la...no, definitely a high "do." There were about five *turones* harmonizing in the deep wok. The aroma climbed the scales, happiness from rung to rung. Can I get one on credit? I wanted to ask, but only managed, "Can I help you roll, Nana Dora?"

"So you want to burn your nose or flavor my *turon* with your grease?" she scolded.

I withdrew the endangered appendage from the wok's edge, along with my grease, or sweat, which I imagined was what she meant. She stared at me, sizing me up in my dress that was once blue.

"I'm just saying hello, Nana Dora," I explained. "If you must know, I'm actually off to a...a business venture." And I'll be earning soon, so can I get one on credit? But the question drowned in the pool in my mouth. I swallowed, but another wave washed over my tongue, my belly made fainting cries, like little notes plummeting, and my esophagus lengthened. "When you feel it lengthen, you know it's really, really bad." Who said that first? Nilo, my fourth sibling, or Junior, the second, maybe Claro, the third one, or perhaps Lydia? There were six of us, so it was difficult to tell who said or felt it first. Not that we called it esophagus then. We just said "it" and motioned with our hands from the throat to sometimes beyond the stomach. Then we squatted for a long time, "to arrest the lengthening." Better than saying we were feeling too faint with hunger to keep on our feet.

"Business venture, hah!" Nana Dora snapped.

Of course she meant, leave business to me, girl, as she

wrapped a *turon* in a banana leaf and handed it to a customer right under my nose. I kept my hand in my pocket.

"Hoy, aren't you supposed to be in school?" Of course she meant, school *is* your business and don't you forget that! But I was unfazed as I listened to the sweet noises behind me—the "ow-ow-so-hot!" then the blowing, then the first crunch, then the customer's masticating. This was how the melody culminated.

"I . . . um . . . stopped school—"

"Stopped school?" Her huge frying paddle—I called it a paddle—froze in midair.

"I'm on my way to some . . . er, business, that's why, but all's well—so can I get one on credit?" My last words were too soft to get me anywhere, but of course she was not meant to hear them.

"Stopped school in its last month, *santisima!*"

It was early March, supposedly the end of my sixth grade and the beginning of a very hot summer. "Yes, stopped school," I said. "I'll be a working girl soon, you know." I pushed out my chest to proclaim my upgraded status. Not that I had anything to show for it yet underneath my blouse.

"How old are you?"

"Twelve."

She stepped back, hands on hips, and squinted at me. "And what happened to your arms and foot?"

I didn't think she would notice. "Accident—cooking . . ."

Nana Dora said something under her breath, then curtly, "Hoy, sit down and help me roll," while the paddle waved

about. She looked angry, but I didn't know why and didn't
care as she handed me the hottest, crispiest, sweetest *turon*
that I ever had in my life. And it was not on credit.

My nose twitched with pleasure, my hand burned, my lips
cooked. I heard the paper-thin wrapping shatter against my
teeth as my mouth pooled and pooled.

three

Shredded heart in coconut milk

"I'm as barren as soup without water, so don't ask me that question again!"

Nana Dora shut me up with this retort when I asked, "Why don't you have children?"

The customers in the queue had heard. Their ears perked up for more juicy details beyond soup and they shuffled closer. Their bodies leaned slightly towards the bristling woman and their faces glowed with the heat from her stove, while the *turones* in the wok performed with more earnestness, believing that they were the object of everyone's curiosity, if not desire.

Her lips thinned. I could see she regretted her little outburst. She tossed more *turones* too emphatically into the wok—the oil leapt and nearly caught my arm. I stepped back, everyone stepped back. I hugged my body to myself, I remembered last night's disaster, I cowered. Fuming, she wiped her hands on her oil-splattered skirt.

"I'm sorry," I said without knowing why.

"Humph," she answered. I was dismissed.

How did we come to talk about soup and stuff? First she

asked me why in the world would I stop school and I wanted to say, because of last night, then she said, there's too many of you that's why, and I argued, but we're only six and anyway Father said it's always cheaper by the dozen, and she shook her head savagely so I said, what about you, Nana Dora, how many do you have, and she said, none, and I asked why, and she talked about soup, spitting her words.

Nana Dora was like jackfruit. Too prickly outside but sweet inside, though only if she was ripe enough to entertain your intrusions. She rarely smiled. Every day she cooked the best and cheapest snacks, except on Sundays. Little was known of her; she did not live in our street or our town. All that was told, again and again, was the story of one early afternoon in the summer during the big drought, when the strange woman arrived and built a makeshift hut on an empty cul-de-sac in our street, then set up stove and wok and pot. She worked with incredible speed. The story went that by five o'clock she had finished building the hut and was grating coconuts, then shredding banana hearts while frying some fish to go with the hearts, then serving her first customers by six-thirty. Why she changed from dinner to afternoon snacks, or from savories to sweets, no one knew.

It must have been the shredded heart, some of those first customers would later surmise. "It was too hot, too salty, too coconuty, ay, too high-pitched in all respects." Even the savories had their place in the musical scale.

"And she didn't know how to shred a heart properly, so we all had the shits."

How to shred a heart.

It must be the right heart, it must be the soft core of the right heart, it must be the yellowish part of the soft core of the right heart. It is this that must be thinly sliced, or shredded if you will, then crushed to let the water out, to bleed it. But how do you flavor a shredded heart? How do you get the pitch right? With a bit of dried fish, a bit of shrimp paste, a bit of little red chili, a bit of garlic, a bit of onion and the milk of one or two mature coconuts. A bit of, just right, not too much, enough to induce that perfect chemistry on the palate. But how can you tell or taste perfect chemistry? When you desire a second helping before you have even finished your first. When the second helping inspires a third. When you don't get the shits after too much inspiration.

So, close to midnight, when the heart is sweet with herbs and spices, it bows from its stem. Wait for its first dew. It will drop like a gem. Catch it with your tongue. When you eat the heart of the matter, you'll never get the shits again—ay, yes, that's more like it. Much later, this state of affairs was revealed to me with unequivocal conviction, or more specifically to my stomach, or to my own heart, or maybe to the space between the stomach and the heart which often suffers that condition called heartburn.

four

Tomato-lemon carp with hibiscus

I never told Nana Dora that I burnt the fish, that Mother beat me as if she were separating the rice chaff from the grain. *Ginik.* What Mother called this kind of beating. Under the ancient two-burner stove, I prodded the welts on my arms and wondered if the skin would come off.

"Only on the bum, Maring, only on the bum, please," Father pleaded. He always pleaded on occasions like this when Mother couldn't see perhaps where to land whatever object she had laid her hands on—his belt, the broom or the large soup ladle dented not from its usual chore, but from carrying out her idea of justice. Anything would do, anywhere would do—bum, back, arms, face.

Under the stove, I gritted my teeth—one is not supposed to cry—after Mother threw the wok at me, burnt fish and all. Spots of oil hit my arms and the fish was like a black hole stuck on my chest, but it was my left foot that suffered most. The oil caught my toes. Only the left foot, only the left, I consoled myself, and not that hot really, compared to Mother's rage. It was always silent but full of fire, like a house burning down. Burnt fish, burnt house. Later, as always, Mother scavenged through the ruins for something "saveable." She sat me down and talked to me as if I were her favorite child. "You know why we hit you? Because we love you. Parents must do this, because they want their children to be good."

But I always want to be good. Do you? I was tempted to return the want to my mother on occasions like this. But before her big blow-up, I'd only managed to explain, in my absent-minded way, "I wanted to cook good, Mama, but it was the fault of the fish." Instantly the house lost its oldest window shutter when Mother grabbed the loose peg that held it together, the closest thing at hand, and began beating me.

Mother's was a poker-faced fury. Her face could have been someone else's, a handsome woman meditating over her laundry or ironing. It was a patrician face: broad forehead, high cheekbones, thin nose and lips, always in appealing repose. Fury occurred only in her hands, as if the callused fingers could not be appeased until they had exhausted themselves. Throwing the wok was more of an afterthought really, a late flick of the wrist.

But why blame the fish? Because its eyes were no longer clear, because its gills were a grey-pink rather than red, because its scales were falling off, but I bought it anyway. It was the only one I could afford with the three pesos (the rice and oil cost two) that Father handed me after he was sacked from his mason's job. After all those salary advances, his last wage was so light on my palm.

It was a weary-looking, passed-over carp, the size of my two palms held together, for a family of eight. Not enough, so

I decided to improvise. I sneaked out of the house while the fish was frying (so now you know why I burnt it) to steal one green lemon, one not-so-large tomato and, in a sudden inspiration, one hibiscus half-bloom from Miss VV's garden next door. I felt no remorse. I took extra care to recite *mea culpa,* while beating my chest as we did at church during the Lamb of God supplications, each time I plucked a needed ingredient.

I only wanted to cook good, I only wanted to *delishusize* the thing. *Delishusize: to make delicious.* I was given to improvisations even then. But how to make delicious a passed-over carp? Scale and clean to immaculateness, rid of all signs of being passed over, the muddy eyes and smelly gills, then rub with salt and fry in coconut oil, fry to a crispness that would surely be percussive in the mouth. Set aside. Now core the tomato. Mash core and save with juice. Slice tomato into thin rings, then lay slices on the browned body. Lay tenderly, like babies on a cot. Then add tomato mixture to the lemon, this sharp-sour fragrance that will hide the passed-over smell of the fish. Only one little green lemon, thumb-sized, so its juice should be extracted to the last drop. Now pour tomato-lemon sauce on the fish. Then grace the dish with the hibiscus, at the right spot where it will curve with the tail. It must only be a half-bloom, it must not be bigger than the fish.

Nothing must be bigger than the fish, especially *not* the stomach. When this aberrant proportion occurs, then we have a problem. But don't we always have a problem anyway? Because desire is bigger than anything that can fill it. Desire is a house with infinite extensions, even renovations, like my little prayer of want after that household conflagration:

"I only want to cook good, I only want to eat good, I only want to be good."

I found this recitation in my head more soothing than "Lamb of God who takes away the sins of the world" while I applied Colgate to my blisters.

My father Gable, so baptized in honor of the Clark Gable and Carole Lombard love-team, quickly handed me the toothpaste after Mother had finished with me. "You'll be okay, Nining," he whispered, eyes averted as if he were the one who had just meted out the punishment.

Nining, not Nenita, for when I was loved again.

five

Lengua para diablo
(The devil ate my words)

I suspected that my father sold his tongue to the devil. He had little say in our house. Whenever he felt like disagreeing with my mother, he murmured, "The devil ate my words." This meant he forgot what he was about to say and Mother was often appeased. There was more need for appeasement after he lost his job.

The devil ate his words, the devil ate his capacity for words, the devil ate his tongue. But perhaps only after prior negotiation with its owner, what with Mother always complaining, "I'm already taking a peek at hell!" when it got too hot and stuffy in our tiny house. She seemed to sweat more that summer, and miserably. She made it sound like Father's fault, so he cajoled her with kisses and promises of an electric fan, bigger windows, a bigger house, but she pushed him away, saying, "Get off me, I'm hot, ay, this hellish life!" Again he was ready to pledge relief, but something in my mother's eyes made him mutter only the usual excuse, "The devil ate my words," before he shut his mouth. Then he ran to the tap to get her more water.

Lengua para diablo: tongue for the devil. Surely he sold his tongue in exchange for those promises to my mother: comfort, a full stomach, life without our wretched want . . . But the devil never delivered his side of the bargain. The devil was alien to want. He lived in a Spanish house and owned several stores in the city. This Spanish *mestizo* was my father's employer, but only for a very short while. He sacked him and our neighbor Tiyo Anding, also a mason, after he found a cheaper hand to complete the extension of his house.

We never knew the devil's name. Father was incapable of speaking it, more so after he came home and sat in the darkest corner of the house and stared at his hands. It took him two days of silent staring before he told my mother about his fate.

I wondered how the devil ate my father's tongue. Perhaps he cooked it in mushroom sauce, in that special Spanish way that they do ox tongue. First, it was scrupulously cleaned, rubbed with salt and vinegar, blanched in boiling water, then scraped of its white coating—now, imagine words scraped off the tongue, and even taste, our capacity for pleasure. In those two days of silent staring, Father hardly ate. He said he had lost his taste for food, he was not hungry. Junior and Nilo were more than happy to demolish his share of gruel with fish sauce.

After the thorough clean, the tongue was pricked with a fork to allow the flavors of all the spices and condiments to penetrate the flesh. Then it was browned in olive oil. How I wished we could prick my father's tongue back to speech and even hunger, but of course we couldn't, because it had disappeared. It had been served on the devil's platter with garlic, onion, tomatoes, bay leaf, clove, peppercorns, soy sauce, even sherry, butter, and grated Edam cheese, with that aroma of something rich and foreign.

His silent tongue was already luxuriating in a multitude of essences, pampered into a piquant delight.

Perhaps next he should sell his esophagus, then his stomach. I would if I had the chance to be that pampered. To know for once what I would never taste. I would be soaked, steamed, sautéed, basted, baked, boiled, fried and feted with only the perfect seasonings. I would become an epicure. On a rich man's plate, I would be initiated to flavors of the finest quality. In his stomach, I would be inducted to secrets. I would be the inside girl, and I could tell you the true nature of sated affluence.

six

Floating faith

Satiation. This was the heart of my business venture that afternoon.

I licked the last traces of *turon* sweetness from my fingers, then proceeded to Miss Violeta "VV" Valenzuela's garden of tomatoes, lemons and hibiscus.

Believe me, there are things that you can't eat, but that feed you anyway. Like VV's red hibiscus hedge. Or like her playing guitar and singing "Yellow Bird Up High in Banana Tree" in her matching pink blouse, shorts and headband, against the red hibiscus. Eighteen-year-old Miss VV was always perfectly tuned in to the most significant event of her Sunday afternoon: the visiting hour of the deep-voiced radio man Basilio Profundo, who read all the letters of request for mostly "croony" love songs in the DZGB dedication program. He especially liked Patsy Cline, Roy Orbison, Paul Anka and Frank Sinatra, playing their songs over and over again so the airwaves threatened a conflagration.

Lovingly Yours was the most popular radio program on our street, not just because of the host's voice made for swooning— everyone was a fan—but for the "uhuum-uhuuumm" that might be brewing between the owner of the voice and the woman of the yellow bird. So, by a stretch of kinship, everyone who lived on our street was related to the radio man. He was, after all, our neighbor's probable "uhuum-uhuuumm." Regularly he brought her twenty pieces of special *palitaw,* still so hot they cooked even their banana leaf wrapping. This always made the air smell like a real Sunday after a long siesta, when Remedios Street steamed, boiled, fried or pounded their own afternoon snacks. When Nana Dora rested.

Unlike the other love-gossip aficionados, my interest in his visit was purely gustatory. I knew too well the banana wrapping that sat on a plate of woven rattan. Basilio Profundo held this plate reverently, like an acolyte bearing the Body of Christ. The *palitaw* was, of course, twenty pieces at least: ten for Miss VV's family and ten for visitors, if she had any. Basilio's mother Tiya Coring, chef of these wooing accoutrements, believed it was shameful not to invite visitors, even sudden arrivals, to share a repast.

Palitaw, the floated one: Tiya Coring's floating faith of pounded sticky rice shaped into tongues and sunk into a pot of boiling water. When they float, they're cooked. This you take on faith. Then you retrieve the tongue-cakes from the water and sprinkle them with coconut cream toasted into crisp, brown granules and, of course, shreds of freshly grated coconut, sugar and sesame seeds. Ay, the scent alone was enough for anyone to take on faith Tiya Coring's claim that hers was the best *palitaw* in the world! And who could argue against her faith in this wooing dish meant to turn not just the heart but the stomach of the doubtful family of Miss VV towards her *unico hijo,* her only son? True, the Valenzuelas doubted whether this man from peasant stock (even if he was a radio man now and perhaps would keep his future wife's feet unsoiled by rice paddies) was suitable for their youngest who was studying to be a nurse. So, twenty sweet, sticky tongues to profess his ardor and honorable intentions.

Ay, to win the beloved on the strength of a tongue. Is this possible?

Faith always floats, keeps us afloat. As it is in swimming, so it is in cooking, so it is in falling in love. We always believe we'll rise to the surface. None of Tiya Coring's *palitaw* stayed down. None remained intimate with the pot's bottom. Faith is too light to stay down, and it smells. We can't hide it.

One day its aroma floated towards our house where myself, Junior (well, Gable Junior actually), Claro, Nilo, Lydia and my baby brother Elvis peeked out of a window about three o'clock. Time to act! I quickly pushed my little brother out the door. Newly bathed and generously Johnson's Baby Powdered by scheming me, Elvis advanced on cue. Go, go quickly, now, I waved to him. Also egged on by four other aspirants, he toddled up to Miss VV while flashing "three" with his fingers: I'm three or may I have three? From the window, we protested with frantic hand signs, gnashing our teeth over the impending loss of a perfect opportunity, or its full realization. Not three, not three, stupid! We are six! But three it was, apportioned with much fighting and tears.

Floating faith made us brave, made us endure the conse-
quences. Before our last mouthful, of course Mother found out.
Thus the interrogation, then justice. I, the shameless eldest who
should have known better, got the belt. Bum, back, arms, face.
"We are not beggars, you hear? We are not beggars!"

Dignity may be lean, but more filling than faith.

seven

Seaweed salad and the Calcium Man
(With *pili* nut husk on the side)

So with faith in my impending business, I walked along Remedios Street, now ringing with the perennial cry of the oldest hawker of clams, mussels and seaweed. "Calcium, vitamins!" Always in English, mind you, like the basic food groups that he lectured his clients about. He knew his wares, perhaps made more pricey in the foreign tongue, and he understood nutrition by heart. My family could not afford him.

It was easy to spot the Calcium Man. He was ancient, stringy and dark like dried fish, and he smelled like dried fish. His hair was a dirty white and he looked as if he had just walked through the eye of a storm. His shirt was torn, his hair stood on end, he had a limp, and he wore no slippers and little flesh. He had no real name. "Perhaps the storm took it too," Nilo or Lydia or Claro once said.

Like Nana Dora, the old man simply materialized on our street one morning, armed with a basket and a temper under his sleeve. He was famous for this temper and for the freshest seaweed, and the clams and mussels that shone like polished stones. He was always early, too early in fact. We surmised that he was a fisherman who gathered his wares before dawn, since he began hawking them by four-thirty, inserting his gruff "Calcium, vitamins!" into our dreams. Or perhaps he was the father of fishermen. But how could those sons bear to have their father slave in his old age? Who would know and who would care? Perhaps the street gossips or the children who still honored their fathers.

I was convinced that his business was flavored by his temperament of the day. If he stuck to his price and haggled with his clients, he would still be hawking dead clams at four in the afternoon. If he allowed a bargain, he would be having lunch by eleven, with an empty basket. He ate under Nana Dora's hut, but always before she arrived.

That afternoon, he was at his hard-hearted best. He believed he was selling a king's ransom. I found him at Tiyo Anding's door, arguing with his wife Tiya Asun or, more aptly, lecturing her on a balanced diet. He perorated about how much protein and carbohydrates the body needed and how indispensable if not lifesaving was his feast of calcium and vitamins.

Tiya Asun had no breasts or hips. Her large eyes had that stunned look of a fish. She had no brows and little hair, perhaps because she combed it too roughly too many times a day, I thought. Her skin was the sallow tint of cornmeal gone off. She always leaned on things, as if they must catch or hold her, but her eyes were vividly alive, "to-ing and fro-ing," her husband used to say.

"Ay, of course you pay a price to save your life, woman—my calcium and vitamins can save your life!"

"I'm not buying, no, not at all. Your price is highway robbery!"

"You calling me a thief?"

"I only speak the truth!"

"Truth! My God, woman! Which truth, whose truth?" The old man shook his fist. He turned to his left then his right, not quite sure which to invoke, the volcano or the church.

At this juncture, I must produce a rough map of Remedios Street, so you can appreciate his gesture.

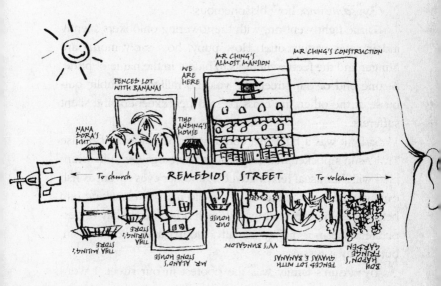

You see, we lived between the volcano and the church, between two gods. The smoking peak and the soaring cross faced each other in a perpetual standoff, as if blocked for a duel. Not that anyone, other than me, saw it this way at that time, of course. Not that I even breathed this vision to any ear, lest I got burnt at the stake or sentenced to recite the rosary for the rest of my life and afterlife.

"I swear by the volcano that my calcium and vitamins will save you, woman!"

"Ay, *Dios ko,*" she shuddered, crossing herself, "how sinful to swear!"

"I swear by God then!"

"Ay, *santisima,* how blasphemous!"

So the fight went on, with the towering onlookers silently judging this earthly duel. How puny, how sadly mortal are hunger and the feeble attempts to hide it in the name of pride. At one end of our street, the volcano rallied for public outburst; at the other, the cross blessed peacekeepers, the silent sufferers.

Sadly it was a fight that could never be resolved, because Tiya Asun's pocket was empty. But she bargained and wrangled with her usual fervor anyhow, and her eyes roved, as fish eyes would, into the basket of the old man, thus making him believe her intention to buy. Ay, such ridiculous futility of desperate pride, no, dignity actually. Mother said pride is a sin, but dignity is a savior.

Tiya Asun's family was the poorest in our street. I wondered what they ate; their house hardly smelled of cooking.

We had been eating more-water-than-rice gruel for a week af-ter my father's and, of course, her husband's sacking. I won-dered what non-smelling thing boiled in Tiya Asun's pots. In my heart I knew that her family felt it too—the esophagus lengthening, I mean. And as they were poorer than us, per-haps even other parts inevitably followed suit—the tongue, the cheeks and the eyes perhaps stretching towards the earth, as if they were already being pulled into their graves. The twins, Chi-chi and Bebet, were thinner than me and wore their mother's fish eyes. We went to the same school. They were al-ways absent from class.

"Go away, you blasphemous highway robbery old man!"

"May your pots and pans break their friendship with pro-tein and carbohydrates and calcium and vitamins and min-erals!"

He did not have to curse her. Tiya Asun had never been friends with the basic food groups. He walked off, still cursing; she leaned against her door. Meanwhile, the volcano smoked, the cross soared, and life went on.

With my burnt toes I limped behind the limping Calcium Man. I imagined I was his sidekick, his Calcium Girl who could also go through the eye of the storm and come out with the beatific vision of the basic food groups. I checked his wares: tired-looking seaweed, clams and mussels, dead by now, and, surprise, something not of the water—*pili* nuts, all black and shiny, and just right for boiling. I looked up to the smoking peak. What if the Calcium Man and I limped to the crater and threw in the nuts to boil? And we could add the mussels and clams that refused all offers for a bargain from the lady who would return to her kitchen to boil air for dinner.

The four o'clock sun was merciless. I could hear him panting and fuming, his limp even more pronounced, making him tilt deeply to the left, as if anytime he would tip over from the weight of his hard, hard heart.

I tagged along, carefully preparing his wares for a meal in my head. First, the seaweed, those beads of jade clustered around their stems. Shiny, firm and a little slimy, they would pop in my mouth like vegetarian caviar. This I would flavor with green lemon and serve as partner to the fibrous *pili* nut husk, dunked in fish sauce. Then I would save the nuts, crisp and with a milky aftertaste, for honeyed crackling or marzipan or palm-sugared sticky delights.

eight

Halo-halo: mix-mix

The Calcium Man did not come too close to his next stop, perhaps because of its vicious menagerie. Four dragons were perpetually breathing fire from its terra-cotta awnings. Any moment now, they could slither down to the main door guarded by a pair of stone lions that never slept, mouths gaping as if flashing their fangs for regular inspection. Then both lions and dragons could advance as a pack through the driveway, past the gardens, to join the company of five live dogs growling behind the red iron gate. And the poor passerby would have to still the shudder in her heart. Well, I did, making sure I kept my distance from the Chings' almost mansion.

Mr. Alexander Ching always refuted any "mansion talk" or speculations that he was the richest man in town, richer than the mayor himself. The businessman was humble or coy, whichever way you looked at it. He went around town in his plain white shirt and faded blue trousers, on foot or in the public buses. He hardly rode in his chauffeured Mercedes and he spoke to everyone. He was always "networking" before the term was even invented.

His almost mansion was an intimidating three-story house

in red, gold and shades of emerald green, built in solid stone. Perhaps it was a fortress that mistook itself for a pagoda. It bisected heaven with a red Chinese turret. The garden, however, was another story. As if in protest rather than contrast, it bloomed in delicate pink—pink roses, a pond of pink lotuses and pink frangipanis that lined the gold wall, which locked in the house from the real world.

"Calcium, vitamins, calcium, vitamins!" The old man had been crying out for a good few seconds now, but was drowned out by the hysteria of the dogs barking and rushing about, snapping at him, fangs bared. They smelled his wares, his heart, its allegiance to the basic food groups. "Calcium, vitamins, calcium, vitamins!"

The sun was right behind the red turret, making it burn like a second, angular sun or some golden talisman that opened briefly and closed again. Shortly a maid came running towards us.

"The señora wants to know whether you have mussels today," she said, holding on to the iron gate to keep the dogs from overturning her.

She was new, soft-spoken, perhaps my age. Her white uniform was too big for her and she was shuffling her red rubber slippers, also oversized. The maid before her had definitely been of generous proportions. She spoke to the Calcium Man while looking at me, perhaps understanding, with my limp, that I was his sidekick, the Calcium Girl who would also go through the eye of the storm.

"Ay, plenty of mussels here, girl, so fresh, so rich in calcium

and vitamins, your señora's teeth and bones will be strong forever and ever."

She giggled shyly at the strange speech, she was new indeed, and studied his wares, then shook her head, saying,
"Dead," firmly, then, "No, thank you, not today, sir." Then she
walked away, flip-flopping her slippers on the pavement.

The Calcium Man was speechless. What insult, what insuf-
ferable offense! Dead! This was the first time in his two years
of peddling that he had been rejected by the almost mansion.
Of course, he was never rejected before because he always
came here first, when his wares were freshest, before he haggled with the rest of the neighborhood and the other streets.
For some reason, today he left the almost mansion for last. But
dead? How dare you? His usually sharp tongue knotted in his
mouth. He could not bring himself to curse the maid, lest his
richest customer overheard him. He looked up; the turret was
closed. The sun had moved on.

His limp dragged him down and he finally tipped over,
falling on his butt beside his basket. The dogs were almost
quiet, perhaps commiserating with the old man's bad business
day. I imagined the dragons would have swallowed back their
fire, if they could, and the stone lions would have turned
away. I did, I was embarrassed for him. The Calcium Man
looked so despondent, as though he had gone through the
eye of the storm the second time around and it had stolen his
spirit.

I was sorry for him, though part of me thought, serves you
right for being mean to Tiya Asun. But what contrast—the

sheer arrogance and even bellicose attitude towards Tiya Asun versus this cowed response to Señora Ching's rejection. Surely I was witnessing the way of the world that afternoon. The poorest are whipped by the poor, and the poor are whipped by the rich, even without them lifting a finger.

What I didn't know then was that the day's bad business went beyond the eighty-year-old's basket, straight to his heart. And that there were other stories which would eventually end under Nana Dora's hut. But I must not get ahead of myself.

I needed to simply proceed to Miss VV's. I refused to have my own bad business day.

"Pssst!" I heard someone call.

"Hoy, it's too hot to be standing on that baking pavement, you'll melt. Come in and have some refreshment—you live across the road, don't you?" The voice had emerged from behind some rosebushes.

I could not believe my eyes and ears, and the Calcium Man was as impressed. It was the only son of the house, Manolito Ching, inviting me in—me, me! Manoling of the tall nose and the long lashes that curved like a girl's and the very thick hair with golden highlights. The Spanish-Chinese *mestizo* (the señora was a full-blooded Spaniard, she even wore a mantilla to church) was the heartthrob of my friends Chi-chi and Bebet—and me, if I owned up to it. He went to the exclusive boys' school in the city. He was the heir to the fortunes of the richest businessman in town. He lived in an almost mansion. He grew up with dragons and lions and delicate pink roses.

His father was constructing the first four-story building in our street. The Chings were going to defy the sky. What more could a girl want?

"Come in."

He had never spoken to me before. He always looked distant inside the chauffeured Mercedes. He barely left the house when he was in town and he was hardly in town. The Chings owned several houses in the city.

"I said, come in."

My mouth kept dropping. I sort of shivered, stammered.

"Good afternoon, Señorito Manoling. I see you so tall and handsome now." The Calcium Man spoke for me, in English. But he was excluded from the invitation, perhaps because he added, "I make you taller with my calcium and vitamins, etc., etc.—wanna buy?" He was hopeless, reducing everything to possible pesos, even this boy's act of graciousness which, of course, kept me from concluding sooner my true business of the day.

So it came to pass that I found myself sitting in the Chings' enormous kitchen surrounded by hovering maids who were shooed away by their master, hell-bent on impressing me with a new gadget. It was a silver ice shaver that one turned with the hand.

He was the most well-groomed boy that I ever saw in my whole young life. It seemed as if everything about him was new: the cream shirt with the maroon basketball print, the brown trousers with their meticulously ironed crease, the cream socks and brown shoes (he wore shoes at home!), even the Beatles haircut which I thought looked like a shiny mop on his head.

"I'm making myself some *halo-halo*. Would you like some? Perfect for this hot day—isn't it just so hot?" He turned on the ceiling fan. His Beatles fringe flew this way and that.

Why me, why me? I felt shabby, ugly and miserably poor. I had to work furiously in my head. I imagined that my dress was deepening into its original blue, whipped into newness by the circling coolness in the room, that my shoulder-length hair was flying softly around my face and my burns and bruises were fading, that I was coming through some storm, much as I had come through the bared fangs of the five dogs at the gate, then the lions at the door while the dragons breathed down on me. Yes, I came through, didn't I, though with much somersaulting in my chest—I was now reborn to a family who would never know how an esophagus lengthened!

"Don't you ever speak?" He was laughing at me.

"Why are you not in school?" For the life of me, I couldn't tell where that stupid question came from.

"School is boring," he whispered with a conspiratorial wink, then opened a cupboard.

I must have sighed too loudly because he looked at me in a strange way.

My heart, with my stomach in hot pursuit, went out to the neat row of colorful jars of preserves that would go into the *halo-halo,* the "mix-mix": orange sweetcorn, red and green gelatin cubes, red and white sweetened beans, purple sticky yam, opaque white coconut balls, raisins, diced sugar bananas and other substances with a psychedelic glaze, which I could not recognize. I was sure I smelled them, in all their competing sweetness, even from the tightly closed jars.

"So do you know how to make *halo-halo*?"

I nodded and went straight for the preserves.

"I'll shave the ice—no, come, I'll show you how to do it."

Reluctantly, I abandoned my original desire and meekly took my place before the silver ice shaver. He guided my hand on the intricately wrought handle, and we began to turn it together. I felt his breath on my nape, and I must have blushed. I was ambushed by the strangest sensations, sweeter than all the preserves in the cupboard combined. Perhaps it was the special detergent of the household: whatever it was, he smelled freshly laundered, with just a touch of something musky. And his breath was sweet mint. I shivered.

"Keep turning," he said, releasing my hand.

Soft frost tumbled from the bottom of the shaver into a crystal bowl. I worked with such industry, I hardly noticed Manoling's preoccupation, or original intent perhaps.

I screamed. Shaved ice was sliding down my back. The devil had slipped it into my dress. "To cool you down," he said, laughing wickedly. "Ta-da-da-da-dah!"

I stopped screaming, uncertain whether I should protest, scold, call him names, walk out, but I laughed with him instead. It was just a harmless prank, a gesture of fraternity to make me feel at home. I laughed louder than the cleanest boy in the world.

"Manolitoooo! Manolitoooo!"

"Aw, Mother-bother!" he said, heeding the call from wherever in the almost mansion, how could I tell, perhaps the red turret bisecting the sky. "Don't leave, I'll be back." He winked one more time.

I was left alone with endless possibilities.

nine

Not quite mixed

Salt, the cheapest of condiments, wakes up the taste of a prime cut of beef. Sugar, up there in status with milk, hops into bed with the humblest tubers. And salt and sugar have been known to conspire, to concoct dishes of the most seductive ambivalence. It's like being neither here nor there; the journey of the palate is tricky.

The journey of life is not any easier. Should I stick to my planned business or stray towards this urgent calling? Should I uphold my mother's dignity or surrender to my mouth's desire? Should I wait like a good guest or should I start discreetly without my host? But the stomach has no pride, and I was left alone with the sweets that had lined up against my soul. I plotted, I argued against the plot, I suddenly felt smaller, diminished. I became my mother's daughter again. Just turn the silver handle, girl, and keep your back to the cupboard, like a true stoic. Or better still, run for your life, made purer by self-denial.

Quickly I was shamed to greater industry by my covetous mouth that pooled in its sticky plots. I made sure I faced in the direction of the church and imagined that I was flagellating my stomach, so it could recover its dignity like a devout Catholic. Pride is a sin, dignity is salvation. I am my mother's daughter.

More soft frost tumbled into the crystal bowl, and above me the eye of the storm turned and turned. But still no Manoling. The frost began to melt; a pool was rising in the crystal bowl, threatening to spill onto the table. And still no Manoling. The almost mansion had grown so quiet.

I stopped turning the ice shaver. I gave in. I went to the cupboard, I examined the brightly colored jars, I examined my conscience. I decided that downfall goeth before pride, forget dignity, and I could live with that. Just one jar, only one anyway, but we'll make it the brightest of all: red gelatin. And only a taste, a little red cube, just one, something that won't ever be missed.

On my palm it shone, it made prisms under the kitchen light. I could see the whirling fan in it; it had trapped the eye of the storm. It slid down my throat, my esophagus, and I imagined it had to travel a long, long way, before it settled quite nicely in that little prideless niche called the stomach. And still no Manoling. So I went for the next jar, the *maca-puno,* the opaque coconut balls scooped from the meat of a special variety of small coconuts that have no juice inside, because the meat takes up all the room in the shell. Much like hunger that takes up all the room in our little shells, our stomachs, hearts, limbs, yes, even our souls. And we walk around wearing the sign, "No vacancy," no matter how high we hold up our chins and smile.

I chewed, I ruminated over my loss of dignity, my shame-lessness and how much belting this would cost me in heaven. Still no Manoling. Next then, the *ube,* the purple sticky yam. My finger struck and stuck. It was the stickiest yam preserve ever. It was the stickiest situation ever—someone had just walked through the kitchen door!

She wore an emerald silk robe with red dragons—she had a penchant for fire-breathing things—and the most beautiful tortoiseshell comb with gold studs, angled gracefully on the side of her low chignon.

She screamed, I screamed, the purple jar broke on the floor. "Thief, thief!" Was that what she was screaming? "No, no, Señora, I'm your neighbor"—"Thief, thief!"—"Your neighbor, Señora, from across the road"—"Wretched thief!"—"Nenita, daughter of Gable and Marina, Señora"—*"Thief!"*

She grabbed my shoulders, she shook me, she was scared of no thief, she was scared of no thieving neighbor, she was scared of no daughter of Gable and Marina, whoever they were. She kept shaking me. The prismed red gelatin that trapped the eye of the storm, the opaque coconut balls that came from a roomless shell and the purple jam that was al-most sinful in its stickiness blended inside me, mixed-mixed with the greatest humiliation of my young life.

The other and real mix-mix, the *halo-halo,* was never served that afternoon. All of life's enduring moments that could be sealed in little jars, all the sweetest preserves mixed with shaved ice and sugar and milk, then topped with ice cream, were a mere melted wish now, brimming from the crystal bowl and messing up the Chings' kitchen floor.

Finally he walked in, muttering, "Aw, Mother-bother!" He looked so clean, so new, so unruffled as he suggested that it was time for me to go home.

ten

Clear clam soup

Nothing could ever hurt me enough to exhaust me. True, that vicious shaking mixed up the comings and goings in my heart, but I walked through the fire of the dragons, the claws of the lions, the bared fangs of the dogs, almost unscathed. Through the eye of the storm and straight to the Chings' construction site, just beside their mansion. It was close to six, I could tell. The volcano was turning mauve, the sky was flaunting dabs of pink and peach. I was almost there. All I had to do was cross the street and head towards Miss VV's house, and my business would come to a close.

I could still hear the dogs barking a parting shot. I should have known better. You don't mix with those above you, you keep to your kind. Culinary tricks, especially the more adventurous ones, never apply to human relationships. My salt with his sugar? Impossible. I thought then that perhaps the rich perspired sweetly and they did not smell.

The Calcium Man smelled even more. I found him squatting under the shadow of the Chings' construction. He wore that end-of-a-bad-business-day look which often came with the salty smell of futility. His head hung like a white-bearded coconut. He was tired and wondering who would buy the dead in his basket. He was picking at his bunions.

"If I had some money, I'd buy them."

He looked up at me and tried to smile. "Ah, you." He knew me as the eldest of the biggest family on Remedios Street. From twelve years old to three: "like glorious steps and stairs," he once said.

"Or I can help you sell them, it's not yet too late."

"Ay, lots of spirit."

The six o'clock bell began to toll. Angelus. A calm descended on both of us, our cares were hushed. He stood up, I straightened myself. We both turned towards the church, then bowed and crossed ourselves. All passersby did the same.

The angel of the Lord declared unto Mary. And she conceived by the power of the Holy Spirit. Behold the handmaid of the Lord . . .

Before us the cross soared, now black against the deepening blue, perhaps like the color of my dress before it was handed down to me by a cousin. The volcano gazed at my back and quietly smoked her understanding. And she conceived strange ideas, which she would spit at us much later, near the end of that hot, hot summer.

The final toll sounded, echoing through our momentarily hallowed limbs, unfreezing us from our prayers. Up and down the street, everyone greeted each other—"Good evening." I took the Calcium Man's hand and touched it to my brow, as was the custom after the Angelus: pay respect to all old people, even strangers, even those whose names we'll never know. All elders are our mothers and fathers, and we must honor them.

I felt slightly breathless, overcome by a deep sense of kinship. The first stars were coming out. In the after Angelus, the world was always kindest. Hearts were repaired, as well as other parts like the stomach and the esophagus.

"Calcium, vitamins!" I hawked through my cupped hands, aiming for the men on the construction's second floor, which sprouted metal bars and scaffolding. Up there, I saw the glimmer of the first fire of the evening.

"May I?" I took the basket from the old man's hand. He did not resist, simply sighed. So, at night, he loses his defenses. I climbed the makeshift ladder. Behold the handmaid of the Calcium Man.

Around a blackened pot, three men gathered. They were cooking rice. I thought of my father and Tiyo Anding before they were sacked. They too would have stared at the communal pot in the growing dark.

"Calcium, vitamins, very cheap and very good for bones and teeth," I heard myself say.

The men chuckled. I noted none were from our street or our town. They were imported workers, cheap labor, perhaps from the barrios.

None of the men could see the state of the basket's contents, nor could the stars up there. In the dark everything could be fresh and alive, if you said so. And I said so. "And you can steam these clams on top of the cooking rice after it boils." To add to your fish, three tiny dried pieces sitting on half a brick.

Money and clams changed hands. Even the dead had a price.

However, on a good and generous business day, these clams would still be alive, sold earlier and without the haggling. They would be perfect for a clear soup, garlicky, gingered, with floating chili leaves and a dash of fish sauce. A bubbly, fragrant concoction that made mothers hum before the stove, that made their faces warm, that opened their tight little pores to allow kindness to seep out and find its way into the pot, onto the table and into the stomach, so it won't ever collapse like our breaking little hearts.

eleven

Smoky coconut chicken in green papayas

At dusk in summer, she always took our breath away, as if to fuel her fire or to help her smoke get to heaven. My brother Nilo, or was it Junior, once said that the volcano's smoke is all our breaths collected, our wish to get to heaven.

When the sky turned peach and pink, the perfect cone changed clothes like a woman not quite sure what to wear for the evening. Blue-grey-green in the day, she became lilac around five, then turned mauve, then a deeper blue-grey, then blue-black, and finally, when the sky was all dark, she stayed blacker than the night. So even on the darkest nights, we could not miss her.

Sometimes stars hovered around her slope. Once she wore the full moon like polished opal, perfectly balanced on her peak. Or perhaps the moon, like a giant head, wore her like a sloping black skirt. It was a spectacle that branded our eyes. We could leave Remedios forever, but we would never leave that momentary twinning of the volcano and the moon. We only had to close our eyes and we'd see it again, a vision that made us believe there is a God.

Against the clear summer night, the perfect cone rose to heaven, guided by a clump of stars.

A JCM bus trundled down the street.

I cut across the asphalt, the *pili* nuts weighing my pockets down. Earned from playing the Calcium Girl, from disposing of the dead. I felt holy, I was happy, I had purpose. I was going to wrap up my business, I was going to be my mother's best girl. I quickly skirted the hibiscus hedge and the tomato patch of the Valenzuelas' garden, the memory of yesterday's crime and retribution marked on my skin. And my thieving soul that inspired a burning.

I could hear Miss VV strumming her guitar and singing about her yellow bird.

The first lines staked her claim to being as bereft as the "bird up high in banana tree." I hesitated—she had a lovely voice. But why must she sing the same awful song over and over again?

Then followed the plaintive query about a friend's departure from the nest, fading with her usual tremolo. Perhaps this, in fact, was my opportune moment. Silently, I rehearsed my lines. I decided on innocent sweetness with enough authority, and with just a slight touch of the "poor me" tone, maybe even a tiny quaver in the throat. My business accoutrements.

As always, there came the declaration of envy, as she sighed into her guitar. The yellow bird can "fly away, to the sky away"—but my knock kept it from taking off. In my head, I inevitably supplied the next line of her song: "You're more lucky than me."

Of course, I knew the song as well as the whole neighborhood did: she sang it all the time. But *Dios mio,* Miss VV—who could be luckier than Remedios Street's most beautiful girl, the only daughter of a doctor and a high school teacher, who lives in a bungalow and who's studying to be a nurse?

"Ah, Nenita. What can I do for you? And how is your brother Elvis?"

"Very well, thank you, Miss VV. Elvis cannot forget Basilio Profundo's *palitaw,* and he says you're very nice and very beautiful too."

She giggled, tossing her head, making her hair bounce—she had so much of it, waves and waves of black undulating to the base of her spine. Her white headband made it look even blacker. She was wearing her student nurse's uniform. White suited her.

"*Aysus,* he's so-o-o cute, just adorable!"

If Elvis could score three floating faiths from her, surely I could do better. "Miss VV..."

"Yes, Nenita?"

Whatever happened to enough authority? "I—I know—I mean, I heard—" Self-diminution is the toughest business.

"Come in, by the way—now, how rude of me."

But I kept my feet firmly by the door. My hands found the *pili* nuts, rubbed them for luck, grateful that her parents were out of town. Then I spilled my intention: "I know your maid left yesterday, I know it's hard to run a household without one, what with you busy becoming a nurse and all that, and your mother and father working hard and all that, so I think you need help badly, your situation is dire, but I cook good, I wash clothes even better, I clean with my heart and soul, I can be trusted, I won't ever let you down—I mean I need a job."

Finally, my business proposition. No sweetness or innocence, no authority and certainly nothing of the "poor me" tone. Just urgency. I couldn't even look at her, and I couldn't tell whether it was her voice or her hand on my shoulder that made my throat tight.

"Is everything all right, Nining?"

When your heart has kept itself from breaking for a while, the littlest gesture of kindness can easily snap it in two. I swallowed hard. There was no dignity in a quaver in the throat.

"Come in, Nining, come in."

She led me to the sofa and sat me down. She noted my limp, she stared at the burns and bruises on my arms. I thought I heard her breathe deeply before asking, "Her again?" In a small neighborhood, most events are no longer news.

"You need a maid," I said.

"No, Nining, you're too young, you're still in school."

"Just tonight, Miss VV, just tonight, I'll cook and clean and wash for you, just a one-off job, just tonight." And you can decide whether you still need my services tomorrow and tomorrow and tomorrow.

"Do they know you're here?"

"No. My mother and siblings are in the city, my father, I don't know, perhaps looking for a job..."

The best thing about Miss Violeta Valenzuela was that she

never pried. She only listened to your stories and, from them, figured out the world in her head. She was very smart, my Señorita VV.

"Okay, why don't you help me cook dinner then, eat with me, and maybe you can clean up after—I have calamine, by the way," she said, examining my arms and foot before heading for the bedroom to get the lotion. "And check the kitchen for whatever you can throw quickly together, I must be at the hospital at nine."

I whipped through the refrigerator, the cupboards. Quick, yes, but not simple. I needed to impress. What would I cook my mistress-to-be?

Tinutungan: "that on which something has been burnt."

Bits and pieces of free-range chicken, especially those that you'd rather discard: the gizzard, the neck, the feet (all those that might make some delicate palates cringe, these are the ones closest to the heart of the matter) and—

> Blood of the chicken
>
> (optional, as I had no time to butcher the fowl myself)
>
> ¹/₂ small green papaya, peeled, seeded; cut to the size of chicken
>> pieces
>
> 1 large fresh coconut, grated for milk extraction
>
> 1 whole lemongrass, tied into a bundle and pounded
>
> 1 thumb-sized ginger, peeled and pounded
>
> 3 cloves garlic, peeled and crushed
>
> 2 green native lemons, halved

1 medium-sized onion, sliced

1 long, green chili

Pinch of salt

I piled the grated coconut into a little mountain. I lit a piece of the coconut shell until it became a glowing ember. In the pile, I made a little niche for the ember. Then I blew and blew through the mountain, careful that it did not collapse. The ember burned, the mountain smoked—indeed a little volcano. Nilo or Junior was right: its smoke is the collection of our breaths.

When the ember died, I threw it away and poured half a cup of very warm water into the smoked coconut mountain. I extracted the milk by pressing the grated coconut in my fists. I passed the milk through a sieve to make sure all solid bits were discarded, and set this first extract aside. Then I poured two and a half cups of the warm water into the coconut pile again. I made the second extract. In our street, we always cooked from scratch, we labored more arduously for our stomachs. Time accommodated our kitchens, our hands accommodated our lives.

I rubbed the chicken with the green lemon halves to disguise the meaty smell. Strange that, all the time, we attempt to make better the smell, taste, texture or look of nature. We cannot leave well enough alone. Perhaps because nothing is well enough alone. Perhaps because the heart of the matter offends the palate, and where it does not offend, it scares. So we arm ourselves with herbs and spices, and we consider ourselves improved as a species.

In a wok, I boiled the second extract of coconut milk, and all the spices and herbs combined (if only I had some blood). Then I threw in the chicken pieces, and when they were half tender, added the green papayas, and brought the mixture to a simmer. Then I poured in the first milk extract before the dish was finally done. I served this with freshly boiled rice, fragrant with *pandan* leaves.

Señorita VV and I sat down to supper. We ate with our fingers. She smiled at me the whole time and asked for a second helping. The whole house smelled of sweet coconut with that comforting edge of smoked things.

twelve

Lab-yu and Fat & Thin
and the rest of my heart's desires

Clutching my very first hard-earned four pesos, a hundred times over I believed there is a God. Señorita VV was overwhelmingly generous. I said I couldn't accept it, it was too much. She said I shouldn't keep her from her nine o'clock shift at the hospital with such arguments, and added that I should quickly wash up and go home. I washed her clothes as well and cleaned the house from top to bottom. I pulled the door shut by about eleven-thirty. There were too many stars in the sky that night, conspiring to be festive.

My business was done. Or part of it anyway.

The last bus had long gone by. I walked to the middle of the road and stood there, turned to the left, then the right. I preened before the smoking peak and the soaring cross. I imagined their standoff was momentarily forgotten. They were looking at me with approbation. Four pesos, more than my father's last wage, and *pili* nuts and a full belly and the memory of the sweetest *turon*—what more could a girl ask for?

It was Friday night and Remedios Street was noisier than

usual. The standby boys were carousing at Tiya Viring's store, trying to outdo Mr. Alano's wailing Cio-Cio San.

Tiya Viring was an orphan and an old maid. Please don't take offense at my bluntness. This is not name-calling, but simply a statement of fact. In our street, we called a spade a spade.

She wore her hair in tight curls; she was tiny, like a girl; she was pale; she always smiled, no, beamed as if she were born to indulge the world. Or maybe it was the other way around: she had always felt indulged by it, what with her eternally munching bits of her store. Sometimes I was tempted to ask whether all her profit ended up in her stomach.

In the next house, Mr. Alano, the artist of Remedios, was always playing something. He was "an animal with the harmonica," and he was not bad with the trumpet and the piano. He was the leader of a band that played at funerals, weddings, baptisms, birthdays and on every Saturday in his own lounge room, in a sort of jam session. He loved opera, also Gershwin and Cole Porter. He smoked cigars, he had airs, he did not mingle much with the rest of the neighborhood. The standby boys hated him.

Every Friday night, at nine o'clock, Mr. Alano ran his fingers through a stack of LPs above his Sony phonograph. Eyes closed, leaving music to fate, he chose the tragic heroine of the night. She sang over and over again at full throttle, er, tremor, in that voice that did funny things to our spines. Next to his house, of course we received an earful with such constancy. We were lulled to sleep by too much wailing.

Tiya Viring kept her store open till midnight. Because she could not sleep either or because she loved the voices of women who sounded as if their toes were being stepped on or as if they just had a big fright, ay, who knows. Tiya Viring began closing up just as Mr. Alano's phonograph slowed to a halt.

Sometimes I hoped his women's voices would cross the street, jump through the red iron gate, past the dogs and the lions and the dragons, then soar up to the Chinese turret. Perhaps the señora would order her husband to lodge a complaint at the mayor's office. It was not neighborly to keep people from sleeping, and certainly criminal to allow frightened women to occupy your neighbors' dreams.

"Hoy, are you waiting for a bus to run you over?" someone yelled at me.

It was Juanito Guwapito, the leader of the standby boys and the youngest son of Tiya Miling, whose store was the archrival of Tiya Viring's. You see, Tiya Miling's dead husband was the cousin of the man whom Tiya Viring jilted on the eve of their wedding, because she caught him with Tiya Miling's youngest sister who was visiting at that time, and Tiya Viring's aunt had actually married Tiya Miling's first beau who broke her heart, which was eventually mended by the man who became Juanito Guwapito's father. Ay, all those little knots that bound the houses in our street could never be undone.

"Hoy, girl, you want to get ran over? But the bus won't come till tomorrow!"

For reasons unknown to all, eighteen-year-old Juanito

Guwapito did not drink at his mother's store. On Friday nights around nine o' clock, he gathered his gang at her rival's. Tiya Miling, all fuming and quivering flesh—she was an ample woman—used to order her son home. This encounter always grew into a big fight over which Tiya Viring beamed indulgently. All that beaming drove Tiya Miling into colossal fits of rage, which she visited on the poor, good-for-nothing Juanito Guwapito. But when she realized that her rival could probably beam her out of her mind, she stopped trying to force her son to come home. She took up the habit of closing her own store before nine o'clock. Tiya Viring's stayed open till midnight, till Mr. Alano's diva finally expired.

"Hoy, Juanito, don't you worry her," yelled one of the standby boys who had whistled at me. "She'll be my girl in the future. I'll grow her up and marry her!"

The laughter of the standby boys, shirtless in the summer heat, made me freeze in the middle of the road. Maybe I should go home, maybe I should just hand over my untouched earnings to my father, maybe he will tell my mother about it when she comes home tomorrow. Maybe she'll think I am the best daughter in the world. But the pull of the palate aching for a sweet was stronger than a grand recognition or even the crass teasing of a bunch of standbys.

Head bowed, I walked to Tiya Viring's store, trying to block out the sniggers of the boys. I fondled the four peso bills. Part of me did not have the heart to break any of them into coins. Ah, the pride (no, dignity) that I would relish when I laid the crisp bills on Father's palm. No, I would not bunch them together. I would watch him smile as I counted out each fruit of my industry. I fondled the bills some more. But my tongue felt coated with too much chicken fat.

"May I buy, please?" I murmured.

We called it chocolate, but it was more powdered peanuts than chocolate, wrapped in a silver tinfoil with "I love you" written on it. My "Lab-yu." Love in a cube the size of a thumb, at one centavo each. Love that stuck to the roof of the mouth as we tried to hang on to it for a little longer before it melted away. And we kept it stuck there, allowing the mouth to pool and swallow, pool and swallow, as we revived our faith in sweet things which, fingers crossed, would not leave us bereft too soon.

"Lab-yu, please, Tiya Viring."

It was only years later when I realized, quite amusedly, how it would have sounded to a foreign ear. "Love you, please," as we handed out our few centavos. As if we were paying cheaply while we offered love, as if its object needed to be bought to receive our affection, not the other way around. No wonder Ralph, the American Peace Corps volunteer, marveled at this little exchange the first time he heard it. But I'm getting ahead of myself.

"Five centavos only, please."

"Can't buy me laa-ab, laa-ab!" Juanito Guwapito teased me, arms fixed as though he were holding a guitar, hips thrust forward, legs apart.

"Laa-ab! Laa-ab!" the rest of the standby boys joined in the chorus. They were fired up with gin and the Beatles.

In the next house, Cio-Cio San wailed and "Can't Buy Me Love" competed accordingly. Tiya Viring beamed.

But I was tuned in to a higher scale. All I could do was order the rest of her lined-up jars in my palate's scale of preferences: sweet tamarind with its slight sour edge, sour tamarind which we sprinkled with salt, sticky and stretchable *balikucha* (possibly as much as two hand spans from the mouth to the pulling hand) made from palm sugar and coconut milk, *tira-tira,* sourish-sweet and also stretchable but couldn't compete with the former, Marie biscuits which we dunked in coffee if we had any, *chicharon* (pork or prawn crackling) which we dunked in vinegar, dry, crackly *galletas patatas* which broke into sharp pieces in the mouth, Choc-nut which was a bigger and more expensive version of Lab-yu, *polvoron* made from sweet powdered milk and margarine and which could choke us if we weren't careful. There were also *turu-talinga* biscuits that came in the shape of ears and lollipops in three flavors, chocolate, lemon and strawberry, which we used as pretend lipstick, plus sweet-and-sour red "hosts," called such by us kids because they were shaped like hosts, though dunked in the blood of Christ, we imagined. And, of course, Fat & Thin.

Now this last one won over the rest. An afterthought purchase? An additional five centavos? I hesitated. Ay, why not, I can still hand over P3.90 to my father.

"Also a packet of Fat & Thin, please," I said. For my siblings when they come home tomorrow.

A fat and a thin man, both dressed in suits and bowler hats, were printed on the packet of salted melon seeds. We ate them with considerable technique and precision, and delicately: with thumb and forefinger, position a seed, pointy side facing mouth, between the upper and lower front teeth. Crack seed, push back with teeth half of the salty shell (mustn't touch lips, or else they'll get pickled and turn white after a whole packet). Now bite out that thin little core.

It was not so much the pleasure from the taste, there was so little of it, but the ritual of eating that kept us going. Too much trouble for some, I realize, but satisfyingly companionable. We always ate melon seeds with company. I loved Fat & Thin. Long ago, when it was just Junior and me, and Mother still laughed, she'd buy a packet and we'd sit around learning these tricks of eating, of companionship, of delight. Ay, she did it so well. There she sat with her patrician features in perfect repose, our melon-seed-eating queen whose lips never, ever turned white.

thirteen

Adobo: the novena of the pork stew

"Where have you been, you brat? Answer me, you good for nothing, *where have you been?*"

His palm landed hard on my cheek. We stared at each other, shocked. My father had never hit me like that before.

My siblings looked up from the table where a stack of greasy plates stood. Their mouths hung open.

He wrung his hands, tried to reach for me. I flinched away.

"We were worried sick. Your mother's still out looking for you. How could you do this to us?"

My heart sank into a bottomless pit in my stomach, my hands and feet developed a chill. I'll really catch it now. But how could I know she was coming home today? And I thought Father wouldn't be back till very late, ay, how could I know. "I—I was just next door, Papa." I found it hard to speak, I had two Lab-yus stuck to the roof of my mouth. "Yes, just next door, Papa, I was busy, so I didn't—I was—I should have—"

"What?"

He raised his hand again before he hid it in his pocket.

"I was working, I was not doing anything bad or anything that you don't—"

"Where did you go after school?"

"I—I didn't go..."

"What?"

"I'm not going anymore."

"What?"

"I'll help you now, Papa."

"What?"

I heard a giggle from the table and someone whispering, "Novena-ha-ha-ha," but for my ears only. Eleven-year-old Junior had quickly recovered from the shock of seeing our gentle father lose control and, like a little devil, was ready to torment me. Or perhaps the teasing was meant to allay his fear. He was now licking one of the greasy plates, while keeping the others from doing the same. "Novena," he whispered again, giggling.

Intention, longing, aspiration, yearning, need, dream, wish, hope, hunger. Most novenas spring from these, which we prayed to the Mother of Perpetual Succor, the Sacred Heart of Jesus, Saint Jude, Saint Anthony, Saint Lucy, Saint Christopher, Saint Peregrine, Saint Martin de Porres, depending upon the nature of our intentions. Each specific personage seemed to have been assigned to an area of specialization. Saint Jude for desperate cases, i.e., to cure lovesickness, Saint Anthony to find lost articles, Saint Lucy against sore eyes and throats, Saint Christopher for a safe journey, Saint Peregrine for those who suffer from life-threatening diseases, Saint Martin de Porres for the poor, and for all other intentions without a specific patron, the Mother of Perpetual Succor and even the Sacred Heart. It seemed we never went straight to God the Father. I used to marvel at His managerial skills. He delegated tasks, all properly categorized in petition forms: the novena.

Why Junior called a severe dressing-down "a novena" was beyond me. Perhaps because novenas had repetitive invocations that could go on for a while, well, for nine days.

"I'll work like you, Papa."

"What?"

"I'll bring home money like you."

"What?"

"And it will be all right."

"What?"

The unlikely invocation went on for a while, until I counted the P3.90 into his hands.

I saw my father shrink, his face cave in, grow shadowed, and my heart nearly escaped from my chest. I shut my eyes tight, waiting for another blow. Nothing, my cheek remained untouched, safe. I was quite confused—true, our hopes and hungers crossed lines if we went straight to God the Father.

By now the Lab-yus had fully melted in my mouth. By now my mother was grabbing me by the shoulder, while my siblings crouched in a corner, horror in their eyes. I did not hear her walk in.

"Ay, Mama, Mama, I can explain, I was—"

Two slaps, one on each cheek, sent me reeling. I hit the table, fell to the floor. Lab-yu, Fat & Thin and *pili* nuts scattered around the room. All the kids scrambled to grab what they could. She seized me again by the shoulders, dragged me towards the wall and slammed me there. Breath knocked out of me, I slid to the floor. She kicked me again and again, then she searched the room for the proverbial rod. I crawled out of her way, but she was quicker. She grabbed the stack of plates and hurled them at me, catching me on the back. I heard the shattering and my chest hitting the floor, then the rain of shards. I couldn't get up, I couldn't breathe, I couldn't cry.

Is it possible that God the Father sometimes hears too late, because of too many crossed lines?

"Why don't you just kill her?" He finally spoke.

She stopped and stared at her husband of twelve years. Still she did not open her mouth. Even now, it is silent fury that I fear most. I felt a strange heat spread at my crotch, seep to my chest and thighs. I had peed in my pants. She left the room.

Father picked up her silence. His words of comfort were devoured by the devil. I felt his hands pressing my back, then lifting my shoulders, trying to raise me. I must have been too heavy, I couldn't get up, as if my chest had tons of lead dragging me down to a bottomless pit that was my stomach.

When I was finally up, I couldn't walk. My legs gave way and he had to lift me to a chair. I couldn't see the trail of blood. I heard Elvis begin to wail and Lydia followed suit. The two youngest wailed out the tons of lead in my chest.

Next door, Carmen flaunted the artfulness of grief. As always, we kept ours simple; we had none of her style. My parents hit me, then fed me, and loved me again.

My father bandaged my back, my mother heated some pork *adobo* for me from the large jar that Aunt Rosario had packed for her in the city. I half understood the origin of the greasy plates. The bay-leaf-flavored stew floated in and out of my daze. My eyes were closed, but I could see the aroma rising to heaven, sending our earthly intentions, all spiced and garlicky, to the God the Father. But who was taking them up to Him? What saint should we assign for this task that we couldn't even begin to grasp? What was it that we actually needed? What was it that we should wish for?

What on earth was this business of supplication?

She made rice gruel to go with the *adobo*. "Eat, eat, it's good for you," she said, spooning my second dinner into my bruised mouth. I heard Father whispering to her my day's expeditions as they went through the rudiments of affection.

In the next house, Carmen had finally expired.

fourteen

The rice conspiracy

Loving and unloving are old conspiracies. As old as cooking. And the secret lies in the collusion of ingredients and the attention of the scheming cook. Every dish is a scheme to appease desire, even rice. Especially rice, this staple that can also conspire against a lesser or less attentive cook. But we have rice-cookers now and their efficient certainty can't be outwitted by the white grains. These will always be cooked just right.

I can do "just right" with my eyes closed, so I have never used those electric things. I can't bear to let a staple sit inside a timed pot that can be left alone. I'm afraid to leave any scheme alone, lest it turns out undercooked or overcooked, or worse, burnt. Lest desire is betrayed, lest the palate falls out of love. I am an earnest cook, especially when it comes to rice.

When I was nine years old, Mother ensured this commitment in her firstborn.

I remember it was the birthday of Aunt Rosario, her only sister. She was our rich relation in the city. She had a big house always smelling of jasmine, except the kitchen. The house had large, airy rooms with barely any clutter. That day in the kitchen, amidst the chopping of every imaginable meat, I learned that all my mother's family were rich relations. *"Buena familia,"* the cooks nodded to each other then shook their heads at me as if I had missed the truth. But how could I know this? I had never met any of Mother's "good family," except sad Aunt Rosario who never married.

On the few occasions when Mother had dressed me carefully in my least faded frock, Aunt Rosario stared at me and sighed, then crossed herself in a sorrowful way as if someone had just died. Always Mother looked away, but with head held higher and chin thrust out. She looked angry when she did this, so I made sure to smooth my hair, then my dress, and to smile up at them. But by then, they had already forgotten me, whispering little secrets in the furthest corner of the room. Strange, in all this intimacy, they never touched. Arms were always crossed against chests, as if something had to be barricaded there. Perhaps the heart of the matter was so precious, it could be uttered only in hushed tones. It was Aunt Rosario who ended up wiping her eyes.

Then to the business of a very busy day.

My aunt smiled at me, saying, "Of course, Nenita can stay till the afternoon, and you should stay too—*they* won't come till tonight for the party."

They were the other rich relations. My mother's parents. So I understood, but only years later.

"Can't stay, but don't worry, I'll come back for *her*." My mother nodded towards me, mocking her older sibling.

"But what about lunch?"

"I brought something."

But you're lying, I wanted to protest. Let's both stay, let's have a big lunch, there's always a big lunch here—

"I said *they* won't come till later, Marina," my aunt insisted, sounding even more dolorous.

"Be good, Nining—and help in the kitchen," my mother ordered before she left.

When it was just me and Mother visiting, the sisters tucked me away in the kitchen. I was meant to help cook, but I convinced myself that really I was meant to graze to my heart's content in the kitchen which always smelled as if God were having a big party in heaven, and the angels in their replete holiness had forgotten to close the doors so the mouths of the whole neighborhood, even on earth, watered.

I still love the indiscreet fragrance of kitchens. They reek with appetite and all its attendant wickedness. Kitchens don't know temperance. They are contagiously improper, well, only the real ones that are able to appease desire, like Aunt Rosario's kitchen. You walk into it and find your flesh afflicted. You leave oiled and spiced, as if you had been marinated in the stew about to simmer in the pot.

That day Aunt Rosario's kitchen had legs of smoked ham hanging like bunting among wreaths of garlic and onion, and sprigs of oregano and bay leaves. And all sorts of meat freshly butchered everywhere, still bleeding and smelling gloriously animal. Then the longest table, surrounded by chattering cooks, spilled with every fruit and vegetable in season, their colors loudly arguing among pounded ginger, chopped onions, garlic, chilies and other spices so strong they made the cooks cry in between morsels of gossip. I listened, I watched, I memorized, I grazed. And of course, I helped cook.

"That greedy girl—always one for the pot, one for the mouth." The portly cook, the grimmest of them all, nudged another, eyeing me.

I pretended not to hear. Of course, cooks must taste their cooking all the time to make sure it works. And I only taste when there's more than enough for tasting to go around. There were five cooks and me intent on preparing the birthday feast for that night.

"But she's getting in the way. Tell her to watch over the rice then, over there, to keep her from trouble." She meant, from troubling them.

"Much trouble for the mother, didn't you know?" And everyone giggled.

As the gossip brewed, getting spicier at each rejoinder, I willed my ear to make sense of my mother's story, but it was all confusing, and painfully so. I was growing more furious by the minute, so I forgot the rice. It boiled and spilled and lost all its water, but by that time my attention was elsewhere. I found it hard to breathe, the kitchen had turned foul and stuffy, and the smell of raw meat rose and rose, fighting all other aromas. One milky eye of a goat's head stared knowingly.

"Rice cooked too soon!" At this, everyone laughed and slapped their thighs. What an original joke.

"She was only fourteen..."

"Disowned..."

"Harsh family..."

"Poor thing..."

"Takes her children here for a feed sometimes. Always hungry, the lot."

"Husband a mere mason..."

"Worthless!" the grimmest cook said, chopping off a chicken's head.

That did it! I sneaked behind her and bit where it was fleshiest. She howled, skipping around in pain and rubbing her bottom, and yelling that I was my mother's shame and sorrow and I stood there under the wreaths of hams and spices, fists to my side like the wrong angel in the wrong party, with God wondering perhaps how on earth a child could afflict a mother so.

Of course, all those little white grains had conspired against me. The rice came out badly cooked, and to my mind at the time, this was why Mother never took me to her sister's again.

"Rice cooked too soon." A curse in my mother's history. Or worse, rice not cooked properly. An unforgivable aberration in the kitchen.

Remember, we have to cook rice in a just right way. First it needs to be thoroughly cleaned. So rid it of stray husks or grit, or toss it around in a winnower to sift out the impurities. Now pour the grains into a pot. Add water, measuring it with the length of the fingers in a just right way. It must be "just right" water. If it's not enough, the rice gets undercooked and hard:

malagtok. Bad for digestion. If it's too much, rice gets over-cooked and gluggy: *marugi*. Bad for the temper.

So like shame and sorrow. Shame comes from being wanting. Shame is thirsty. And sorrow? Well, sorrow is runny, always painfully wet.

fifteen

The soup of stones

"Babies come from the armpit."

Was it Nilo, the third, or Claro, the fourth, who made that stupid prognosis? Ay, I always forget. Perhaps I need some point of reference, a clarification of our steps and stairs. Me, twelve; Gable Junior, eleven; Claro, nine; Nilo, seven; Lydia, four; Elvis, three.

And my mother was not even thirty.

Mother ate like a rich woman, of course. She hardly opened her mouth, she chewed delicately, took small helpings, held the spoon and fork lightly. I gripped and clunked my cutlery, ate with my hands. I slurped, I spilled, I chomped and spoke even when my mouth was full. Sometimes she looked at me as if I belonged to someone else. I did not have her graces. Was this the cause of her shame? I often wondered then.

Grace is twofold, you see: a given and a later gift. First, the given, that genetic boon, like Mother's very fair skin, and her high cheekbones and fine nose which I sometimes traced with my fingers in my dreams. Mother is a beautiful woman. Imagine planes and angles that make dramatic shadows before the stove. Mine are rounded, uninteresting. Facially, I am my father's daughter, moon-faced and snub-nosed. I am dark and all inadequate and uneven roundness, something like a heart, something that never comes gracefully full circle. I can never make her happy.

And grace as a gift? Ah, those little manners that are bestowed on us as a child, if we are bright enough to learn them. Manners evident in our most basic preoccupations like eating, where I have always betrayed myself, exhibiting my hunger. Have you? Don't you, in whatever consuming gesture you choose to put on? When you pick, stab, shovel, masticate daintily or audibly, lick lips and fingers or dab them on a napkin, look or not look at your food and proceed with the machinery of ingesting as a matter of course? Do you know your betrayal? Do you know hunger?

Forgive me. The last question is out of order. I should know better. Hunger we all experience. Hunger is the greatest leveler of humankind, if it wishes to be leveled. But how and whether we appease it always restores the social order.

My mother's marriage to my father had collapsed the social order beyond restoration. The rich relations in the city, except her only sister, did not wish to know about their kin who ran away with a mason during her first year at high school. Much later, it was Aunt Rosario she'd run to, but only when the more-water-than-rice gruel became our staple for weeks.

It took a long time before Mother gathered enough humility to beg for help. Humility was like those scraps of rice that she picked from the bottom of the pot and saved for the next pot of gruel. Don't get me wrong. Humility was not about loss of dignity, she told me once. Her kind of humility, which saw her running away to the city with her brood (which never included me after the rice disaster), earned them wonderful meals which they boasted about for days. Of course I knew these meals and how I missed them.

During those seasons of humility, reserved only for her sister, Mother's rage ran away from her hands into territories that, perhaps, even she had never imagined. My father, the once dashing Gable, got lost in her rage. First he lost his words, the devil ate them. Then he lost his footing, walking on eggs around the house, an impotent man whose only recourse was to clean up after her rage, to bring her stolen flowers from someone's garden or to hold her tightly at night, whispering over and over again, "I love you, Maring, I love you."

Then a baby always arrived from the armpit.

But I shouldn't promote my siblings' silly speculations. I should tell you more about my father. What he did on that night which shattered on my back.

Aquamarine, ocher, white, grey, magenta and a red one with black ridges. All beautifully smooth stones, except for the last one. He found them after he ended up on the beach just outside our town, after a futile afternoon of job hunting. He brought them home. He said they reminded him of his six children. Aquamarine for Lydia, because she had the gracefulness of sirens. Ocher for Nilo, because he was like the earth when it caught the sun. White for Elvis, because his laughter was clear and pure. Grey for Claro, because he was as somber as a stormy sky. Magenta for Junior, because he was like blood with wicked secrets. And the unsmooth red with its black ridges was me, because I had fire with the promise of burning.

Maybe this was why Mother ran away with the mason and his threadbare clothes: he looked at things closely, tenderly. He tried to know them by heart. Thus exposed, this strange organ must have fascinated her once, having been born to a family that never hugged. I heard her parents were scarily formal, a couple of staunch believers in unbending discipline, which meant withholding all traces of warmth. Discipline was like rice, the staple of their children and served cold. Always refrigerated and thus preserved. Never retrieved from the cold lest it went off and punished their own stomachs for the rest of their lives.

Father knew his wife by heart, "with its soft, soft core." "Putty," Mother often replied, especially after their third child, when Father ambled through each crisis in that perplexed, helpless way.

Putty. Each time Mother spat out the word, I remembered the grimmest cook's summation. *Worthless*. Echoed by a knife falling, severing the chicken neck.

"Come home with flowers, come home with stones? Your children can't eat them!" And Mother always pulled out of his embrace.

In my family, we never hugged. We loved each other in our own way. He bandaged my back, she fed me *adobo,* and that settled the evening, then we all went up to the ceiling. I didn't know about ceilings then. I just thought we had a special bedroom where no one could stand except Elvis.

It was past midnight. Mother confiscated what was left of Fat & Thin, but Elvis would not let go of the last Lab-yu. "Eat it tomorrow," she said. "Now you must sleep. Today was too long." Then she rolled out the mat from end to end of the ceiling and opened a little vent. It was a very hot summer. Our sweats commingled.

"Prayers now," she said.

We never hugged, we did things together. We called out to God as one. We lay our bodies as one. We closed our eyes in unison or some of us pretended to. Maybe we even dreamt as one.

Prayers over, he kissed us good night, handing each of us our special stone.

Strange how a little thing like that has stayed with me for a long time. To this day, I have not forgotten our sleeping arrangement, because I cannot forget the order of stones.

RedwithblackridgesAquamarineGreyMagentaOcherWhiteFatherMother—vent

I could not lie on my back, it hurt. My siren sister faced me, singing siren songs in her wide, wide eyes. She could not sleep, I could not sleep. In the dark, she touched my cheek with a finger and found it wet. Next to her, the storm shifted uneasily for a while, before it snuggled as close to us as possible. But the blood with wicked secrets kept himself turned away, seeking solace in the earth that caught the sun, who'd rather dream of clear and pure laughter, which clung to the waist of our father, who clung to our mother and whispered, "I love you, I love you," while she kept her face turned away, breathing precious air from the vent.

It was a very hot summer. Our sweats commingled, we smelled as one. Into the wee hours of the morning, I fondled all our stones in my head. I looked at them closely, tenderly, and put them together in a magic pot. I imagined we had become the soup of stones.

the spleen of the matter

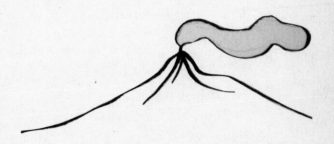

sixteen

Bittermelon graced with eggs

Once upon a time, the bittermelon was sweet and not frowning. It was a shiny, smooth green of the palest hue, with no creases at all. It was a fruit, not a vegetable. It was served for dessert. It was sweeter than mangoes but less fleshy, and it was lean with character; it did not give in too easily to the teeth. People ate it as they would eat corn, gnawing around and around the elongated green flesh, crunchy and sugary sweet, till it was naked, white and vulnerable-looking: a collection of teeth marks. Thus exposed, it became ashamed of itself. Time and again, it worried that its underbelly, with such a savage imprint, would be seen by human eyes and judged. So it began to flinch each time it came in contact with teeth, any stripping teeth for that matter. And each time it flinched, its smooth skin tightened, creased a bit, like a worried forehead. Then each time it worried, its sweetness diminished and an acrid taste crept in its place. With this shifting flavor came a change in color: it slowly darkened. By the time it turned a deep frowning jade, it was struck out of the dessert list. It had become a bitter vegetable, fallen out of favor with most palates, pushed to the culinary fringe.

The fringe is probably the best way to tell the story about the last Saturday afternoon of my free life, when I was sporting a bandaged back. Allow me to begin with Boy Hapon's fringe garden.

Boy Hapon was and was not part of our street. He had never left his garden during the twelve years that I'd known or heard of him. I think he was afraid of us, and we of him. Our street decided long ago that he was not quite complete in the head. I never saw him, properly that is, only glimpses of him if I climbed the highest branch of a guava tree in the lot next to his garden. On this large lot grew guavas and bananas. Here was our territory, where I came to play with the twins Chi-chi and Bebet, and raid the guavas, of course. Our guavas leaned against the high bamboo fence that closed off Boy Hapon's world, which was shaded by a huge mango with an unusually long branch. It extended like a bridge towards the guavas, it invited us to trespass. On occasions we tested it and peered down: no sign of habitation, except, on closer look, a hairy green animal crouched in a forest. This was actually Boy Hapon's hut sprouting vegetables of all kinds, the bittermelon most evident of all. From our roost, we saw how this vine flourished the whole year round, dangling a shiny, frowning fruit from every corner like a testimony of worry.

And we heard chickens, no, the whole neighborhood heard and believed he had chickens. They crowed through dawn, from about three to seven, and too many times, much to the consternation of our dreams. We never saw them though. Like his hut, they were buried in edible greenery. For years I imagined he was the only one in our street who would never, ever grow hungry should the world come to an end.

On that Saturday afternoon, for an hour we imagined tales sprouting from Boy Hapon's vegetables. From the guava trees, my friends and I looked down on his garden, playing "I spy" and "Once upon a time." The fragrance of lush greenery assailed our noses, it made our toes curl.

"I spy something with an *s*—"

"*Sitaw!*"

"Once upon a time, Juan climbed the tallest *sitaw* vine, so tall it reached the sky where a snoring giant son lived with his snoring giant mother."

"I spy something with a *b*—"

"*Bataw!*"

"Once upon a time, Juan sneaked into a *bataw* pod, pretending he was a seed, and slept there forever, close to mother and father and brother and sister seeds, well until the world came to an end."

"Something with a *p*—"

"*Patani!*"

"Once upon a time, Juan ate a *patani* bean and began to speak in *patani* tongue that no one could understand, not even his mother or father, or brothers—"

"Ay, so unappetizing!"

We were bored. We had to spot the least obvious vegetable below and tell a story about it. Both vegetable and tale must whet the appetite. But all we found were beans, those creeping legumes that inspired slow-legged tales of the traditional folk hero, Juan, who never went anywhere beyond the first sentence. Our storytelling powers were arrested too soon. Chichi and Bebet, who had been stripping off the fruit (ripe and otherwise) from all the guava trees since lunch, rolled their eyes to heaven and said that they didn't like beans at all. "Ay, they taste so-so, you know." I kept myself from retorting, "But how would you know, your house never smells of cooking." I felt mean that day, my back hurt.

"What happened to your back?" they had asked the moment they saw me.

"I fell from the sky."

My back hurt, my back was interrogated, my back told a tale in five words, and that was that. The twins knew my tale was going nowhere, even if they sensed that its plot would thread all my obvious bruises and the slow, funny way I conducted my limbs that afternoon. But they commiserated accordingly and felt honored when I allowed them to examine the bandage (Mother's oldest skirt) and to feel it, but gently, gently. Their awe reeked with guava. Their mouths were forever engaged, munching then whispering their admiration over and over again. "Ay, truly magnificent!"

A child always wears the mark of disaster with bravado. It feels heroic. In my case, I believed I was an embellished star. Mother's skirt was floral.

The true story of my back could have perked up our lethargic afternoon, but my lips were sealed. In that humidity, our boredom ebbed and flowed with halfhearted inventions instead.

"I spy something with an *a*—"

"Amargoso!" Bittermelon.

"Once upon a time, the bittermelon was sweet and not frowning."

So we return to where we began, the bittermelon and our street's fringe-dweller, which I can no longer evade. I tried to as I took you through a day's tour from Nana Dora's hut, thinking I could go home without speaking about Boy Hapon—Boy, the Japanese, who was so pale it seemed he'd been stripped of his first skin, or did I only imagine that? Sometimes I was convinced that the paleness flashed around the greenery, like a dapple of light. I never saw the teeth marks though, well, not then.

"Imagine not having a mother, a father, and brothers and sisters, and grandfather and grandmother, and cousins and such," Chi-chi said, plucking the last bunch of unripe guavas.

"Well, he's an orphan, what do you expect," I said. My friends and I decided long ago that he was someone our age, and alone.

"He is just him, just him and no one else." Bebet repeated the old line of the street gossips. "He has no surname, no ancestry, he did not come from anyone."

How was that? He did not even come from an armpit?

It was two in the afternoon and our street was having its usual siesta. Earlier I had sneaked out of our bedroom where only Elvis could stand. Not that anyone was standing when I tiptoed out. Everyone was a casualty of last night's disaster. The shock, perhaps the guilt, and the last of the Lab-yu and

Fat & Thin (fought over by my siblings) had all been consumed. My family was tired and spent. Me? I did not need a siesta. I was on top of the world, on top of the guava trees, the summer sun on my floral back. Nothing could ever exhaust me.

A JCM bus with a lone passenger trundled past in its own drowsy way.

"Hoy, what in the world does he eat?" Chi-chi asked, greedily munching two unripe guavas at a time, with the third on the ready.

And what do you eat? I bit my tongue, hating to embarrass her—she was making him sound like an alien from some far-flung planet. What does he eat? Hoy, look at his garden, stupid!

"So what does he eat?" Bebet joined in.

"Isn't it obvious?" I snorted.

"I bet it's bittermelon for breakfast, lunch, dinner—yuck!" Chi-chi cringed, stuffing the last of the guavas into her mouth.

"What do you mean, 'yuck'? At least he has breakfast and lunch and dinner!" I couldn't help the contempt sneaking from my throat, akin to a burp's sourish taste. Look here, I wanted to say, Boy Hapon eats, my family eats, I don't know about yours—and I helped my family eat. I earned and Mother fed me *adobo* and Father made his soup of stones and all's sweet again—but I couldn't tell them that.

"Bittermelon, yuck!" Bebet persisted.

"Of course he eats other things or can't you tell?" I scolded, the sourness sharpening my tongue. "You fools, he has his garden, his chickens—"

"I think we just dream he has chickens." Bebet's response was as sour.

"And chickens have eggs," I said, angry now. "And eggs make bittermelons taste good."

"Yuck!"

"Eggs and tomatoes and garlic and a bit of shrimp paste."

"Yuck!"

Want is bitter, graceless. It disparages those who have the power to appease it in themselves. The underbelly of unappeased want is even worse. Envy is twice bitter, and bitterness is an acquired taste.

seventeen

Upside-down and inside-out cake

To sweeten the tongue, we climbed down the guava trees to where only sweetness was conjured—the most cultured house in our street, the house that did not believe in siestas.

It was Mr. Alano's Saturday jam session with his band. It was Mrs. Alano's session of exotic confectioneries (she owned an American cookbook).

Believe me, that Saturday was their session of all sessions. I realized then that sweetness, at its most insistent, could be as grave an assault as gnawing bitterness. It could as easily cause our faces to tighten, crumple, and the rest of our bodies to follow. Inevitably we could become a walking and breathing frown. This is very bad for digestion.

By the time my friends and I had ambled to the two-story stone house with carved awnings, it already smelled like caramel, but laced with tobacco. In the kitchen, Mrs. Alano was perhaps browning the sugar, while her husband's big band primed themselves with cigars. Through the shutters, we could see and smell them, poring over their instruments in the lounge room, getting "tuned up" for the afternoon. And surprise, Basilio Profundo was there too with a radio assistant, both looking anxious among their recording paraphernalia. Outside the crowd grew restless in the summer heat resonant with anticipation.

No, this crowd did not smell the rumor of caramel. Apparently, the day before, they had tuned in to Basilio's *Lovingly Yours* dedication program, and were promised that today's program would be recorded in our street with singers from Manila. Imported singers! Not exactly heart-stopping, of course, like the presence of the host himself in his official capacity as radio's "true voice of love." Truly, everyone was a fan of Basilio Profundo's baritone, which perused his listeners' love letters in such perfect timbre, so their ardor became more lofty, their anguish more grave.

The radio idol could not sit still, repeatedly looking at his watch then at the door. Still no singers or singer, just one, actually. But yesterday he couldn't resist the plural slip of the tongue to impress his fans. Manila's finest voices were dying to be on his show.

The lounge room seemed to expand, roof and walls pushed by large-fisted notes. The clarinet cleared its pipes, the oboe obliged in turn, the saxophone sailed forth a reply and the trumpet traipsed around the double bass busy double-dealing with our hearts, tu-dum-tu-dum-tu-dum, while the drums dropped in and out like some dabbler or doubtful visitor. All the while Mr. Alano, consummate musician that he was, hopped from harmonica to piano to electric guitar, his latest acquisition.

In the kitchen, Mrs. Alano whisked the eggs.

Summer was hotter than usual. Outside, fans, hats, cardboard scraps, even rags, waved in and out of conversations.

"Who are the singers, do you know?"

"Is it a he or she?"

"*They,* stupid!"

"Isn't he just so charming, ay, look at him with his microphone."

"Wait until he speaks."

"Then he'll teach them the meaning of charm."

"Then all those blowing mouths will learn to keep to their place, hah!"

"Did you see one of them take off his false teeth before blowing?"

"Lest he swallow them with all that strain."

"I hope he reads a love letter."

"I doubt it. I suspect this is just singing and blowing those stuff, ay, what a pity."

"I hope those singers are good then."

"Of course, they're imported!"

Basilio Profundo had been clearing his throat and intoning, "Testing, testing, one, two, three," to his microphone. He was growing extremely nervous. He had sent a friend to pick up the crooner hours ago from her hotel in the city. She had no taste for small towns, and she was already a good hour and a half late. His eyes shuttled from microphone to door. As yet, it only promised a deluge of oglers and hangers-on.

Mr. Alano was raring to shut the door. He could smell sweat, he could hear the ignorant asides. "How much longer,

Basilio?" he asked, playing the first bar of "Rhapsody in Blue" on the harmonica. "Is that singer of yours coming at all?"

Meanwhile, Mrs. Alano was perhaps pouring the caramel into a cake tin, tipping it here and there so the sweetness could spread evenly. She smiled to herself, she hummed a love song, she imagined a deep voice dipping into this amber lake, burnt just so for that added bite. She was a closet fan of the radio man, her adulation locked in lest her husband mock her pedestrian taste. She was no opera or Gershwin or Cole Porter buff, and she swooned over sticky-sweet declarations of the heart. She liked them as "trickly" as caramel just off the pan. How much longer, Basilio?

Outside I was asking the same question. I needed proof, the reason for all the talk about a voice that did extreme things to the chest: shortness of breath, accelerated heartbeat, bursts of heat, and all that stuff the ladies spoke about in hushed tones.

"Ay, like a volcano heaving in your chest!" someone said.

I looked up. The smoking peak was a shimmering blue-grey-green, grand as ever. No, she would not bend that low, I wanted to retort.

They were all there, siestas cut short for an urgent cause: Tiya Miling and Tiya Viring (they never missed a single *Lovingly Yours* program), Tiya Asun (she always listened on Tiya Viring's radio), other women from other streets, even young, giggly girls my age (but I'm not one to giggle), and of course the twins making guava-breath mists on the windows. But not my mother. Our family did not own a radio.

"I don't think she's coming at all," Mr. Alano said, puffing his cigar while running the second bar of Gershwin on the piano. He had okayed this music assignation, even if he felt nothing but contempt for *Lovingly Yours*. He needed "some exposure, the long awaited career break." He could be discovered in the airwaves, well, why not? He was tired of funerals and weddings and birthdays and such. He had always found them demeaning anyway, what with his prodigious talent. "So are we recording or not? I don't have forever, you know," he added, bearing down on the keys with such authority that the band was silenced.

Mr. Alano's hair glistened with Three Flowers pomade. The greyish, flat plain was a landing pad for the afternoon sun streaming through the windows. Basilio Profundo was as thickly pomaded, but his hair had natural waves that poured towards his forehead. A thick, slick curlicue of hair, which bounced each time he moved, hid a deepening frown.

Mrs. Alano was unlike these dandies. Her tight curls were unbound, like a cloud of well-whisked egg whites framing her face. She had white hair and a still-young face. Untouched by the escalating anxiety outside her domain, she was now laying slices of pineapple all over the lake of caramel, including the sides of the tin. This would not only be an upside-down but an inside-out cake as well. She had decided to improvise: the caramel-coated pineapple should be displayed all around the cake. Sweet truth exposed! Ah, but what she would have done to find glazed cherries and walnuts. But we make do, this is not America. She looked at the glossy picture of the exquisite upside-down confection on her imported cookbook and sighed.

At this juncture, our poor radio man was saved. Not that the singer from Manila ever arrived (we never knew what happened to her and the supposed escort, though there were rumors that are better left off this page). It was Miss VV who arrived instead, walking into the lounge from her rounds at the hospital, still in her white uniform. She had come to watch her suitor perform.

All the men stood up, and those who were standing sort of inclined their heads in acknowledgment. She had this effect, you see. Mr. Alano instantly revived Gershwin's rhapsody on his piano, harmonica, then his electric guitar. Radio man dropped his voice even lower as he whispered, "Lovingly yours, Basilio Profundo" to his microphone. One of the horn players discreetly took out his false teeth. Then the clarinet, the oboe, the saxophone, the trumpet, the double bass and the drums came alive in a thunderous harmony. We had to cover our ears. Tu-dum-tu-dum-tu-dum, the men's hearts went, in a beat so low it echoed down to somewhere lower than the stomach, circled in that spot which I couldn't name, tu-dum-tu-dum-tu-dum, before it wandered all the way to their very soles.

Basilio rose to his feet, suddenly inspired. "Maybe, she could sing?"

Of course, she could sing, but does she know any other song? Almost everyone had heard her "Yellow Bird" countless times. "She could learn, she's a natural." Basilio leapt to her defense, hoping to ingratiate himself with his heart's desire, and to save the day, of course. "That crooner's a good two hours late now, and VV's heard this song so many times, I'm sure she'll do it beautifully—please, VV?"

The song in question was the radio program's theme. In fact, it was Basilio's love letter to his beloved student nurse, whom he had met at a friend's party and impressed with his deep-as-a-pool voice. After that meeting, he always signed off his program by playing the love letter: Patsy Cline's "Crazy." Now, its lyrics suddenly materialized from under his shirt (what, he even wore them?) and were handed over to the flustered captive as the band meandered through their introductions. It happened so fast, we were not quite ready for what followed.

In the kitchen, Mrs. Alano stopped short before her oven, cake tin in hand. Is that the singer from Manila? Is that a record? She rushed to the lounge, uncooked cake still in hand. She sat in a corner. She rested the cake on her lap. She could not return to her kitchen now. A tiny strangeness had curled in her stomach. Something was turning upside down in her house, its innards revealed, pale and waiting for the inevitable teeth marks to show. Brow furrowed, she stared at her husband, playing his guitar too close to their flushed eighteen-year-old neighbor. It was one of those moments of illumination.

He has never looked at me that way, not even on the day we were married.

Tu-dum-tu-dum-tu-dum.

Quickly Patsy Cline found her voice. Patsy Cline grew crazy. Patsy Cline flaunted her incredible throat, rich with slurs and quavers and never-before-heard vibratos. She was a natural indeed, a sweet crazy. Mrs. Alano was certain her performance was sweeter than the caramel at the bottom of the tin.

eighteen

Biniribid: the twisted ones

Begin with black rice: *maragadan*. It is as dark as its name. *Maragadan*: like death. Pound this to powder. Mix with brown sugar, not-so-young coconut meat and a bit of water. Mix till it becomes a thick paste. Now take a handful: stretch, fold, twist. Deep-fry in very hot oil. Then roll in sugar. Serve.

This is perhaps true of all of us. Stretch the patience, fold the spirit, and the disposition gets twisted. But it is never served sweet like Nana Dora's *biniribid,* the twisted ones. Another snack which is like pretzels in appearance, before pretzels became too ornate. The *biniribid* is of a wondrous consistency: crisp on the outside and soft and sticky inside with strips of coconut surprising the teeth. Its aroma is that unforgettable earnestness of deep-fried sugary things. And the taste? Pure delight. I miss it.

Nana Dora, however, had a way of dampening delight. *"Pag nagkaon ka ki odo kang saday, matitipsikan ka— maturon iyan!"* she explained.

In the dialect, it hits the perfect eschatological timbre: "If you ate feces when you were a baby (something that some babies do unwittingly, of course), you're bound to get burned by hot oil when you grow up!"

"*Aysus,* cooking *biniribid* has its risks, you know." Nana Dora showed me the dark-brown spots on her chest. "Burns," she explained. "I must have been a naughty baby."

I could not get over her culinary aside. How can a delicacy bear tales that make the stomach turn? How can it hold so much portent? Delicacy and darkness—or delicate darkness?

The hot oil hissed, the black-rice-like-death twisted.

"Don't dismiss it, it's true, and don't look at me like that."

I laughed to cover up my doubt, or was it discomfort?

"Hoy, it's not funny, Nenita, I wear the scars on my chest."

I was back at Nana Dora's hut under the blooming banana hearts. I had to tell her about the strange musical event across the road and the fate of my earlier business venture, concluding right outside Mr. Alano's house. That was the last Saturday afternoon of my free life.

I craved for sweetness to mark the event.

Chi-chi and Bebet had tagged along. I felt encumbered. I could probably score only one free *biniribid,* but the twins' eyes went this way and that, and I knew the look. I wondered how much their combined esophagi had stretched by then, and whether the distance they covered was at all measurable. I would have to share my loot then (if I was successful, of course).

I foresaw good tidings the moment we arrived. The look on Nana Dora's face promised a hundred percent success rate.

"*Dios mio,* what happened to you, Nining?" Nining, not Nenita: a hundred percent and no less. "Ay, ay, what happened, child?"

"I fell from the sky."

When she cupped my face rather brusquely, I nearly spilled the story of my back and my bruises and the strange, funny way I conducted my limbs. But it was only a five-word tale. I could not give Chi-chi and Bebet the satisfaction of seeing tears. "I fell—"

"As the cross is your witness?" Nana Dora asked.

Towering above our heads, it perched like an admonition on the burnished dome. I could not swear by it.

We stayed that way for a while. Nana Dora looked me in the eye, I looked back, didn't flinch one bit. You see, I never lied, I only told stories. When she finally released me, she humphed and harrumphed before saying, "Okay, help me twist."

We understood each other, we understood dignity. I'll earn my stomach's keep with honest labor and surely Mother will approve. So I positioned myself as far as possible from the spitting wok and began to stretch, fold and twist. The twins followed suit. We all earned our twisted repast that day.

Thus ensconced in a hundred percent success rate, I could finally tell Nana Dora *the* story. But a hungry queue trickling from the event across the road drowned out my intention in a cacophony of gossip.

"Ay, that Miss VV has the voice of an angel."

"I didn't know Mr. Alano could sing."

"Did you see the look in his eye?"

"Did you see the look in Mrs. Alano's eye?"

"What about Basilio Profundo?"

"Ay, isn't he such a he-man *na* he-man?"

"And that deep, deep voice, *santamaria,* I could listen to it forever!"

I must clarify this grapevine, before it cramps my own storytelling. This was how it went: Patsy Cline met Roy Orbison.

The student nurse, in her white uniform that so became her, crooned to the microphone and to Basilio Profundo (or so he thought) and to the guitar-playing Mr. Alano (or so he also thought) and to the whole band (or so they all thought), even to Mrs. Alano, who felt her life was summed up in that first line.

Ay, to grow crazy "for feeling so lonely"—what a curse.

After their children grew up and went to study in Manila, leaving their parents in separate bedrooms, all loneliness was sweetened in Mrs. Alano's kitchen. Here, she cared not for the grief of opera divas, but for getting the egg whites to stiffen in her homemade ice cream or for making sure the chiffon cake rose on time and the muffins browned just so.

Then Patsy Cline declared the possibility of love, albeit eventually lost.

At this juncture, Mr. Alano drew even closer with his guitar. Patsy had to focus extremely hard on her performance to refrain from giggling, so she played along to his amorous chords, fluttering her eyelashes at him (or so he thought).

But then, of course, the departure "for somebody new" followed in a Patsy sigh.

Suddenly Basilio Profundo was filled with foreboding. He saw the performers' little flirtation. Was that departure someday meant for him? He grew hot around the collar, his gut twisted. He wanted to call off the recording. He wanted to punch Mr. Alano!

When the song concluded, Mr. Alano said, "How about a male voice then, another love song to add to your repertoire?" The events were escaping from Basilio's hands, he could not say no to his host. So Mr. Alano took center stage and began "Falling" in true Roy Orbison style. It happened so fast, I couldn't make sense of it.

Roy even decided to kneel before the sofa where Patsy sat, unable now to restrain a giggling fit.

Outside we went crazy. We didn't know they could sing so well. Our palms smarted with too much clapping. Ay, we felt proud. They were our neighbors.

Then the pall descended before Roy and Patsy could attempt a duet. The recording broke up on the wrong note. I smelled the discordant air.

Mrs. Alano disappeared into the kitchen, the cake unsteady in her hands. Mr. Alano returned to his piano, but not to finish Gershwin's rhapsody. Basilio Profundo steered Miss VV out of the house, but with a most morose face. His hair curlicue had lost its bounce, his frown was exposed. His gut could not untwist itself.

Outside Miss VV saw me and stopped in her tracks. She looked me over, especially my back, and my life was never the same again. She said she would talk to my parents. She said I could start work the following day.

nineteen

Piko-piko, sinanggarito, pinalupag, cinusido
(*Piko-piko*, the chiled dish, the coconut dish, the soup)

The day I became the maid of the Valenzuelas, Mother stopped looking at me. I swear her smooth forehead developed a crease which, like everything else, she wore with grace. I couldn't bear to watch the humbling of my parents.

In the tiny square of our one-room house, my father looked even more tiny and angular. But my mother stood tall and poised, though she could not do anything about the angles; she was just built that way, all sharp edges. Señorita VV, with her gentle persuasion, softened the air. I fell hopelessly in love with my new mistress then. Not with her beauty, everyone had already fallen for that, but with something I couldn't yet comprehend. From the corner of my eye, I did not see an eighteen-year-old who giggled and blushed before the falling Roy O. I saw someone older, more composed, knowing, and the voice I heard was rich and rounded, like life that had come full circle. Kindly, it asked my mother, "So when is it due, Manay Maring?"

"End of summer."

"My father knows a midwife who makes house calls, we can get her for free, I'll talk to her—"

"No, thanks."

"It's—it's rather small."

"I know."

Father turned to the wall, staring at his hands. The devil had eaten his words again. He imagined the women's voices were heavy with accusation. A seventh one? His face burned.

No wonder she sweated more miserably that summer. How could I have missed it? How tight did she bind it? Perhaps I wanted so much to miss it. We were all of six already and we were always hungry. But fate was designed by Elvis. What did the old folks say? "A baby who sucks his toes means his mother will soon be pregnant again." Elvis always sucked his toes, ay, stupid, stupid Elvis.

"*Sige,* pack all your clothes, Nenita," Mother said.

"But she can come home every weekend."

"No, keep her."

There was a pause in the room. Do you know that the heart can actually pause? That there are pauses between heartbeats?

Then Señorita VV sighed, and my father left the house, as always, silent.

I went to the ceiling to pack. They were all there, ordered to stay put until the conference downstairs was over. My siblings stared at me, opening their mouths and closing them again, as if all the words they conjured inside were not worth airing. I could tell that they already knew.

"Hoy, don't look at me like that, I'll just be next door."

"I'll work too, you'll see, and I'll get rich before you do, just you wait, I'll be better than you are, and I'll be eldest now, ta-da-da-da-dah, and you can't boss me around again!" That was Gable Junior. Magenta: wicked blood.

"What will you buy me when you get rich, Nining?" Nilo: ocher for optimism.

Claro was more than somber sky. He was all snot. Meantime, my only sister followed me around with siren songs in her eyes and air through her missing front teeth. "You vithit, I vithit, you vithit—"

"Of course I'll visit—don't be stupid, Lydia! Hoy, listen up all of you, I'm just next door!" I looked at them, crumpled and faded like hand-me-down children.

"Pa-taw, pa-taw." Elvis was tugging at my dress, six fingers raised.

Palitaw: floating faith. Faith always floats, keeps you afloat. Well, Elvis got it right that time. I assured him Señorita VV could spare six pieces from Basilio Profundo's regular offerings (if he would still offer them after yesterday's event).

"And more than *palitaw,* I'll bring you much, much more," I said, suddenly inspired. "I'll score you *pochero, lechon, mechado—*"

"And even fried chicken, beefsteak, and lots and lots of it?"

"Sure, lots and lots."

"And Lab-yu?"

"Of course—*sige,* tell me more, tell me more," I chattered, launching into our usual food game of *piko-piko,* where the leader invites all the players' forefingers to dip into her open palm as she intones a folk rhyme:

Piko-piko
Sinanggarito
Pinalupag
Cinusido . . .

Meaning, *piko-piko,* the chilied dish, the coconut dish, the soup . . . and it can go on and on. The other players chant additions to the list of dishes, until the leader quickly shuts her palm as she calls out, *Pusit!* (Squid!), hoping to catch any forefinger not agile enough to withdraw in time. Of course, the players can hold back her concluding "squid" by reciting a culinary litany.

For a long time that afternoon, Junior kept my palm from shutting, kept me from packing my clothes, kept all our hungers at bay with his chant of mains to desserts to snacks, remembered from visits at Aunt Rosario's in the city, and now echoed by every mouth in the room, amid much laughter and teasing—

morcon	pork roll with chorizo, egg and raisin stuffing
tilmok	hot shrimp, crab and young coconut parcels
afritada	thick, spicy tomato beef stew
estofado	beef in spicy liver sauce
otap	thin sugarcane biscuits that crackle in the mouth

barquillos	milky crispy biscuit roll
linukay	palm sugar sticky rice with sweet anise
hinagom	toasted corn balls with young coconut strips
kalamayati	sticky rice with coconut milk and honey

I was not allowed to end the game with such unimaginative fare as squid. We wrapped our tongues around so much food that day, we feasted. So when Mother told me to hurry because Señorita VV was waiting downstairs, we were in good spirits again. Our mouths had pooled together—the soup of stones, but very soon, minus the unsmooth red with black ridges. They'd be all right, I assured myself. They'd do better without the fire with the promise of burning.

twenty

Green mango salad

Pregnant women ask for sour things. Pregnant women ask for stolen sour things. Pregnant women must not be let down. It is bad for the baby.

I blamed the myths. Before that summer ended, I blamed my stupid faith in myths. Pregnant women must not be let down? But what if the touching ground, that ungraceful nose-dive, came before pregnancy? But myths break a fall, they keep us afloat.

Faith, or is it fatalism? Ditch responsibility; blame it on the pregnant body, as in the case of the myth of *lihi,* which conspired with unripe mangoes and the crowing habits of Boy Hapon's chickens. This configuration came to pass after almost a month of my being the "most hardworking maid ever."

My employers were more than generous. Dr. Valenzuela treated my back, Mrs. Valenzuela and her daughter, my heart. It grew fat with their constant praise. "Ay, Nining, your smoky coconut chicken is number one!" "You're such a hardworking girl." "The garden is looking absolutely neat and the plants are happy, thanks to you." "I have never seen floors this shiny." I didn't know what to do with too much approval. At the end of the day, I always felt replete but restless, like when you eat too much dinner and can't quite digest it. I couldn't digest all the meals anyway. For the first few weeks my trysts with the toilet came with painful constancy. My little stomach was perhaps shocked with such abundance or was constantly fretting about the other five next door.

I missed their racket—Junior's wicked teasing, Claro's whining, even his snot, Lydia's demands for attention, Nilo's endless queries (What's for lunch? What did you bring me? What are you chewing?)—and the smell of Elvis's toes. I missed the way Father looked at me, at us, always closely and with unequaled attention, as if nothing in the world mattered except the moment of looking. And insane as you might think it, I missed Mother's heavy hands landing on me, especially the change of heart that followed as she sat me down. "We hit you because we love you."

Mind you, I charged her rage to *libi*. A pregnant woman can irrationally like or dislike someone or something which is the object of her *libi*. This dislike can be extreme, mercilessly splenetic. Like, on the other hand, can be almost amorous. Usually it is an obsessive desire of the palate for mostly sour things. She must have them, even if you have to steal them; she might even prefer that you steal them. Once, rumor had it that Tiyo Anding stole a green mango when Tiya Asun was pregnant with Chi-chi. "Certainly not!" Chi-chi protested when the story was told. "Father bought the mango and Mother knew from the taste that it was bought!"

See, there's a "bought taste" and a "stolen taste," and these knowing women can tell the difference. Such acuity of the palate.

"And she ate it and it didn't hurt one bit. Look, I came out okay."

"No, you didn't, Chi-chi. You're always grazing among the fruit trees."

That summer I was twelve, *libi* made sense. Mother vented her spleen on me because she was pregnant, and she couldn't help it. Today, twenty years later and so far away from home, I understand, and I forgive.

And the green mangoes? They're number one in a pregnant woman's list of desires, or so the myths said. Well, actually, one doesn't have to be pregnant to desire them with that irrational pooling of the mouth. Green mangoes, even just the mention of them, made our mouths water. We ate them plain with salt or shrimp paste, or in a salad with tomatoes, onions and again shrimp paste or fish sauce. This salad is the best partner for greasy dishes. The crisp sourness combats the fat, cleans the tongue.

Mother's tongue did not need any cleaning (she was a pristine woman), and she never begged for green mangoes. But I had to steal them for her as a peace offering. The voice of the grimmest cook from that rice disaster day had branded me: I was my mother's shame and sorrow. I had stolen so much of her dignity, she often said. I needed to compensate for my crime with another act of theft.

My business had not concluded after all. I was not yet my mother's best girl.

Stealing the mangoes was easy. Close to my guava roost, there was the mango branch that reached out like a bridge; there was an invitation to trespass. I took it.

I made sure I was alone, with no twins rolling their eyes to heaven. I made sure it was a Saturday, siesta time. Señorita VV was singing at Mr. Alano's jam session, and Dr. and Mrs. Valenzuela were in the lounge talking about an American who was visiting soon. The talk was punctuated with yawns and words slipping away, because they had eaten too much of my chicken *adobo*. Soon they were snoozing longer than usual in their room. Perhaps the bay-leaf-flavored stew induced somnolence; even its fat slept, coagulated.

So I found myself looking down from my guava roost, sure I was alone. Through the mango tree leaves, through all the edible shrubs and vines, I spied for that flash of paleness. Boy Hapon was nowhere to be seen.

Now this mango bridge was sturdy, and tried and tested. Perhaps too many times. That was what did it, I must say. You walk all over something too many times, you wear it down, it snaps. I never snap, I only fall from the sky—but who would ever think that I had foretold my fate?

With a bunch of green mangoes, I fell straight into the arms of the palest man I'd ever seen. A vacant pale, like paper that you want to quickly write on. We stared at each other, and I held my breath. No, he was not a young boy as we had suspected from his name. I took in the lined, longish face with high cheekbones, the eyes that sloped upwards and the very big ears.

"You'll h-have long life," I stammered.

He chuckled and gently put me down. Now, why did I say that? Because big ears mean long life.

"You want long life?" he asked.

I was suddenly fearful. This wrinkled man whispers, this man is "not quite complete in the head," this man has no father or mother or siblings and such, this man did not come from anyone. This man is a ghost.

"I—I'm sorry—accident, just accident . . ." My voice trailed away. I stared at the mangoes at my feet, debating whether to pick them up and whether to run away after picking them up.

"If you want, ask."

I could barely hear him. He had already left me before I understood what he'd said. He speaks after he leaves: I made a mental note. Maybe this is how ghosts make conversation. I felt a sudden chill despite the summer heat. The green forest, dominated by so much frowning fruit, was closing in on me. Once it was sweet and not frowning. I picked up the mangoes and broke into a run for the gate.

"If you want, ask." I heard it again, and he wasn't even there. I stopped, deliberated, and felt ashamed of myself. Even ghosts must be thanked.

I walked back, holding my breath, past the *sitaw, bataw, patani, pechay, kalunggay,* mung bean, yam, tomato, onion, garlic, lemongrass, cassava, sweet potato, radish, squash and other gourd things, all incredibly robust and watered with human blood and harvested under the full moon when witches were abroad and dogs were howling as if someone had just died ... By the time I reached the green, hairy animal that was his hut, I had already told myself a ghost story.

I found the ghost sitting in a one-room affair, smaller than ours, made even smaller by piles and piles of Mills & Boon romance books where five chickens roosted.

twenty-one

The flavored tale

Perhaps the chickens crowed according to the flavor of the tale. From three to seven in the morning, when Boy Hapon could no longer sleep, perhaps he read to this huddled mass of feathers and beaks. Perhaps their crowing was an exclamation of pleasure, of wonder, of anxiety or despair, or of whatever leap in the chest occurs when you're rapt in a love story. I knew about Mills & Boon then. I often saw Tiya Viring reading this stuff while munching a sweet or a sour snack, whichever was suited to the flavor of the tale.

Every story has its own taste. Every storyteller has her own taste; so does every listener. So when I speak in a particular flavor, I know my words taste differently on your tongue. While it is the ear that receives a story, the main event happens in the tongue repeating it, a contention that was proven right among the guavas and bananas.

It was a week after the mango incident and I was having an unexpected tryst with my sister Lydia who, at my departure, had summed up her hoped-for routine: "I vithit, you vithit, I vithit—" "Of course we'll both visit," I had agreed. But none of my siblings were allowed to visit.

She had probably slipped out of our house unnoticed. There was no following recall of the truant—psssssssssssssst! A cross between a hiss and a screech, loud enough to be heard throughout the whole street. I often wondered how the mouth could have so much authority, how it could cause so much dread. Psssssssssssssst! This was how Mother called us back, if we suddenly slipped out to "gallivant," with her whip of sibilants that sent us running home, a scared thump-thumping in our chests.

But Mother was not home that day. I was sweeping the Valenzuelas' garden when I saw Lydia walk past. The fraying green shirt (Claro's shirt, but a midi dress for her) tentatively stopped among the hibiscus, then walked on again to our territory. She had seen me, she had allowed herself to be seen by me, but did not call out. I followed her. I did not call out either.

We went past the guavas and ended under the canopy of banana leaves, their hearts in various stages of bursting: a purple skirt lifted here and there, a yellow filigree exposed like some lacy slip, a row of flowers uncurled like diminutive legs. This is how hearts open, often shamelessly.

"You promith vithit," Lydia said, her tone accusing, though without the full authority of the sibilant. She had squatted an arm's length away. She was folding and unfolding the hem of her green shirt, her eyes on the ground.

"I did visit, didn't I?" And I brought *adobo,* smoky coconut chicken, and even *palitaw* one time, as Basilio Profundo had not yet lost heart.

Now a next-door visit is always done with pleasure. To go neighboring is to bring good tidings, especially if we're celebrating something, say a birthday or a christening. We drop by with portions of our feast. Or we just pass that hot plate across the fence, saying, "Taste some of my special so-and-so, because so-and-so turned ten today." Usually the receiving neighbor feels embarrassed about returning a clean plate, so it must be filled with her own cooking.

We took neighboring seriously in our street. My mother, even more so. I sensed how she cringed whenever a plate was passed over the fence by Miss VV, because of some occasion or other. Mother smiled too brightly as she said her thanks. I always returned a clean plate.

"I did'n thee you," Lydia said, face and fringe askew. She was right. She did not, could not see me. Mother made sure of that. "You did'n vithit." Her eyes threatened me with siren wails.

I looked up, I made her look up. "Ay, Lydia, there'll be hundreds of bananas here before summer ends, see? I'll cook some if you want—what dish would you like?"

She grew serious, looked about then looked at me, still worrying the hem of her shirt. "You bad," she sniffled, then breathed deeply, as if drawing strength from her lungs for the next accusation. "You thteal . . . Mama theth."

There was hardly any strength there, but my sister kept at it: You steal, Mama says. I did not know how to decry my mother's judgment.

"You thteal?"

The act of retelling has more clout, more truth, than the act of hearing. Told again, a tale in fact gains conviction, the belief that it is worth telling and that the telling is worth our while.

"You...bad?"

"Of course. I can steal all those hearts if I want to."

"Ay, I tickle!"

"And I want to." I tickled her armpits again, her nape, the little dip on her back, sending her squealing.

"I tickle, I tickle, ay-ayyyyy!"

It was like old times. I could smell her still-baby smell and we were suddenly back on our mat in the ceiling, my red with black ridges next to her smooth aquamarine, then the grey, the magenta, the ocher...I missed the sleeping together.

"You thmell nithe...uhhmmm..."

I smelled of my employers' kitchen, of cooking, of abundance. Ay, this perfume of food. My sister sniffed my hands, my cheeks. It was the closest thing we got to kissing. Feeling awkward, I turned away. "Is Father working now?"

She shook her head. She grew serious, we both grew serious. We looked up at the green canopy and their bursting hearts blocking the summer light, keeping us cool.

"Juth little bad," she said, trying to decide how little was little in the space between her thumb and forefinger. Then, "Thith little," she finally said, drawing her fingers together so only a sliver of light could pass through.

In my ear, her toothless declaration had the flavor of sweet things, or of things only about to be sweet, like bananas before they are fully born.

twenty-two

Stillborn banana fritters

I went neighboring with little success. Mother cringed each time I came with a plate from the Valenzuelas. I couldn't stay long enough to see my siblings, because she asked too many questions. How she preached without looking at me, her eyes at the door as if she were already leading me out even before I had laid down my offering. Do my employers know about this plate? Am I sneaking out food from their cupboards? Should I not concentrate on my work and stop playing truant? Were they not paying me for my time? "Work with dignity, girl, and stop gallivanting!"

"A gallivanting whore!" Her family's bruising admonition when she fell pregnant by a mason. She never got over the bruising. She remained pale even in the hottest summers.

She used to tell this joke about paleness or about melons, whichever way you heard it, and her lips would curl but not in a smile.

A melon farmer, passionate about his melon reputation, was hawking his produce around a village. One sweaty midday, this reputation was severely tested. He had just declaimed about his sweetest-reddest melons ("unlike those pale pink run-of-the-mill ones"), but someone had doubts and thus chose one for too long a time, knocking at each fruit, putting it close to his ear as if the green rind promised an oracle only he could divine. The farmer grew impatient. After a good fifteen minutes, the customer chose the tiniest melon and haggled for a mean bargain. The farmer was angry by this time, but eventually gave in. Just as he was leaving, he heard a horrified cry. The melon had fallen on the road and had split in two. No, the horror was not from the accident, but from the treachery that met the customer's eyes—the melon was a very pale pink inside! Not red as the farmer had promised, and possibly not sweet at all, oh no. So the customer demanded his money back, but coolly, the farmer replied, "Believe me, sir, I only grow the sweetest-reddest melons, but if it was you who had fallen, wouldn't you grow as pale?"

After a fall, one can bleed inside. But some do worse than bleed. Their blood is scared away instead, along with its sweetness, and they remain pale for the rest of their lives. They lose color in this strange internal bruising.

Mother never got over it. She fell pregnant and fell out of her family's favor. I suspect she never wanted the pregnancy, but my earnest young father knew that a baby would make sure she couldn't leave him, and she never forgave him or me. Her shame, her sorrow.

Nowadays I often wonder whether I scared her blood away, and whether, for the rest of my life, my true business is how to coax it back. And whether, once, she had also wanted to scare me away. Whether she had bound me as tightly as her seventh fruit.

But on that Sunday when I went neighboring, she had already allowed herself to show and we had other fruits on our plate. I was bringing her the stolen green mangoes, she was peeling sugar bananas. Cobbled green with black warts and plucked before their time. Ugly, stillborn.

I wanted to ask where they came from and whatever could she do with them, but remembered I was there to make peace. I held out the mangoes instead. But her eyes refused to leave her chore. She was peeling with some difficulty; the bananas were mostly all skin. So I laid my offering on the table and asked, "They're upstairs?" I moved towards the ceiling, but she stopped me.

"Your siblings are resting, don't disturb them."

"And Father?"

She laughed, derision evident. "Somewhere dreaming for a job."

"He tries."

Again she laughed, saying, "I know."

"He does...I do..." I whispered to myself.

Tomorrow, I'll win her back. Tomorrow.

Her hands labored. The knife cut through each thick, cobbled skin and found only hard fruit inside.

I stared at her back. As a younger child, it was my favorite pastime. Studying her back, memorizing it, especially how beautifully her nape swept to where her hair began when she had it up. How pale the skin, how smooth like white cucumber. But that day, I noticed how lower down the smoothness was marred by the bump of—was it the bone? Mother was so thin and so pregnant.

I moved closer, smelling banana sap and bereftness, hers or mine, how could I know, and my arms ached to encircle her and her seventh fruit, wanting to croon to it that everything will be all right and that we can coax it back, her blood, her look, her sweetness, but she flinched when I came too close.

"I brought you green mangoes, Mama."

Later that night, while preparing green mango salad for my employers' dinner, my stomach heaved upwards, threatening to replace my heart, to spare it from the nasty pricking that is what scares the blood away. After a fall from anyone's grace.

She accused me of stealing the green mangoes. She said I was a thief, a shame to our family; she sent my offering back. Perhaps what she meant was I shamed her own stillborn meal that day: the *sinapot,* the banana fritters.

Sugar bananas sliced in thin halves and gathered in five slices for each fritter by a mixture of slightly salted rice flour thinned by water. Then each fritter set on a dried leaf of *madre de cacao* and deep-fried to a golden brown. Always urgently sweet and starchy to the smell and taste.

Urgency perhaps, but none of sweetness and often compensated for by earnestness. I remember them now, my mother's condiments. Ay, how she wanted all of us to eat and eat well, nagging each measly meal to multiply in her desperate hands. Even bananas that did not have any hope of bloom in them.

twenty-three

Hot coconut guava

Is it a fruit, is it a vegetable?

Of course, guavas are fruit, you might say. But not always. The nature of a thing is realized in the intent of its user, a principle that does not preclude human beings. For instance, I am only as good as my use to you, in this case as storyteller, as rambler of recipes, as reminiscer of sensations, as the older version of a bewildered child. But not quite old enough to escape this humbling state of bewilderedness, this daily ambush by life's divergent exigencies. Is it a fruit, is it a vegetable?

As fruit, guavas can be eaten half-ripe, crunchy and sour, with a bit of salt. Ripe, they will do plain, without salt, but watch out for the consequence of those rose-pink seeds, the sweetest part. "*Ay, mahamis na Kalbaryo*—a sweet Calvary!" Bebet once exclaimed. Because eating the sweetest part, especially too much of it, means an agonizing internal journey in the lower regions, like that mythical descent into hell. Such is the nature of constipation most dire.

Too ripe, guavas are definitely much safer. It's easier to chuck out the seeds. Then we decide how to eat it. As a sweet or a savory? A fruit or a vegetable? A jam or a chilied dish?

If we choose the latter, again we must employ the proverbial coconut milk (my town couldn't live without it) plus garlic, shrimp paste and long, green chilies, the hottest that you can find, to prepare a perfumed savory—you see, guavas have a peculiar fragrance, strong and rose-pink. When I smell guavas now or imagine I smell them, I see rose-pink, that ball of countless tiny seeds inside the yellow-green flesh, that sweet conjurer of constipations. Imagine this scent countered by the pungent aroma of shrimp paste, also pink, but with the hue of bruises. Imagine a dish so hot, your mouth can burn.

Chi-chi did not know about hot coconut guavas, though. How could she? She never allowed guavas to grow ripe. To her, the guava was first and foremost a fruit that must be plucked and quickly consumed. I was ashamed of her hunger, of the way her eyes rolled round and round and up to heaven, as they scoured the guava trees with the intent to plunder.

But on that stickiest day of summer, her eyes were elsewhere and my eyes just followed hers.

Across the road, in front of their red iron gate, Manolito Ching was dribbling his basketball, wearing a pair of navy blue silk shorts, white socks with blue piping and, of course, blue-and-white sneakers. The shorts were very short indeed, with a white number nine inscribed on the right hem. To us, the Chinese-Spanish *mestizo* still looked impeccably groomed, despite his sweaty bare chest. The golden highlights of his Beatles mop lit up even more. We ogled, he flashed his dribbling skills. Inside the gate, the five dogs of the almost mansion were as excited by the dribbling.

"Ay, so *guwapo*—so handsome." Chi-chi elbowed me. "Don't you think?"

I thought of the aborted *halo-halo* some weeks ago, of the ice on my back and the fan whirring above, sending my hair flying this way and that—"I've got to go, the rice would be just about cooked."

"Uyy, you can't look at him." She grabbed at my arm.

I recoiled, perhaps echoing my mother's response the other day. So this is how a bruised fruit feels. "What d'you mean?"

"You like him, don't you?"

I crossed my arms tightly and turned away.

"Go on, call him," she giggled.

The vision of well-being at its peak was too much to bear, but I managed to sound indifferent. "I'm working, you know—you call him."

"I dare you."

I felt my cheeks burn.

"Aha, she does like him!"

"Calcium, vitamins! Calcium, vitamins!"

Saved by the Calcium Man. I settled down a bit as I turned towards the road again, pretending I was searching for the hawker. Nowhere to be seen yet, but his wares were already branding the air. I calculated the time and his temperament. Surely he had haggled again through several households, so lunch would be late. Under Nana Dora's hut, of course.

"I hate that stingy old man, really so stingy—ay, really so

handsome, go on, call him!" Chi-chi had an annoying way of shifting gears.

I willed my eyes to leave the bare-breasted boy and said, "Goodbye," ready to run, but—

"Hello, girls!"

None of us could move before the perfect teeth at the other side. His preening and our ogling crossed and recrossed the road, and better sense was ambushed by hormones. We were a very young love tableau, fixed between a church and a volcano.

For a moment, a JCM bus and an old Ford filled our view, then the heart-stopping smile again and something close to a cleft chin. Chi-chi and I often disagreed on the merit of the latter.

"How are you, girls?"

Even his English was impressive, "so slang *na* slang," meaning it had an American twang, and that was supposed to be wonderful.

"Hello, boy!" Chi-chi answered, also in English. Ay, so gauche. You don't say, hello, boy!

"Calcium, vitamins!" The other English speaker was just limping into view with his usual basket.

Manolito Ching finally crossed the road, dribbling the ball towards us, and Calcium Man reached the red gate, announcing his wares with more aplomb. The dogs went wild. The red gate opened, the girl in white uniform examined the proffered basket and money exchanged hands. I felt relieved for him.

"*Kumusta*—hello!" I called out. The old man waved and winked at me, then poured all the contents of his basket into a white basin which the maid held gingerly. I imagined live clams and mussels and jade green seaweed.

"Catch!" someone said, then I felt something hit me and I nearly stumbled.

"Hoy, why so snobbish?" he asked, coming close to pick up his ball. "I'm Manolito Ching."

"We know," we both said.

"And I'm Chi-chi and this is Nenita."

He had sent me away without even asking for my name.

Chi-chi was all over him, gushing like a plastic bag with an irreparable hole. Charm and more charm escaping. When she smiled like that, she lost her contrary look. She became quite pretty, eyes crinkling at the corners, mouth softer. But the bare-breasted boy was looking only at me, or so I wished, though I hated to admit it.

"*Kumusta*," I said coldly, and turned to go. I refused to speak like him. We did not speak in English while shaving ice in their kitchen, and only the richest families spoke in English or Spanish at home anyway. Manolito's family spoke both, and they used the dialect for the maids.

"So hot, isn't it?" he reverted to the dialect, because of my current station (but what would he know) or because I had put him in his place with my snobbishness. I had no wish to find out. I turned to go, confused at the sight of moist rose-pink nipples. He was much taller than I and was standing too close. Ay, that musky smell.

"Oh, don't go." He laid a hand on my arm. "Let's play ball."

"Let's," Chi-chi said, not missing his familiar gesture. Her smile had lost half its luster.

"I'm busy," I said, unable to withdraw my arm, which prickled with goose bumps. Perhaps this is how fruit awakens to its ripening. This little sweet shock.

"Schoolwork?" he asked.

"What do you mean?" Chi-chi answered for me. "She's actually working."

"*Sige,* see you soon," I said, hastily walking off.

He blocked my way, dribbling the ball before me. "Just for a little while?"

I stared at ebullient confidence. All gleaming *treinta y dos* exposed, as we'd say. Thirty-two: the full set of perfect teeth again.

Chi-chi grabbed my arm. "C'mon, just for a little while."

I allowed myself to be led or I lagged behind as the two got engaged in serious talk. Animated, Chi-chi looked very pretty indeed, despite her rag of a dress. She had by now grabbed his arm (she had a way of grabbing arms) and was guiding him towards her guava trees. She was even whispering things to him. I stopped in my tracks, embarrassed at her effusive display. What an easy girl that Chi-chi is, I told myself. Something twisted in my gut. I could see the heir of the almost mansion nodding and Chi-chi smiling her crinkly smile to her fullest capacity of prettiness, until we reached the guava trees.

Quickly my best friend ran true to form. She could not help

the instinctive gesture. Her eyes went round and round then rolled to heaven, scouring the trees, plunder in her heart.

"Let me climb it for you," Manoling said, letting go of the ball. First the dribbling, then the scaling of trees; next it would be mountains.

Chi-chi and I looked at each other. Of course, we both knew that there was hardly anything up there today, even if she hoped otherwise. We knew our guavas. But Manoling was set to flaunt his gallant intentions.

Suddenly Chi-chi was shaking in a strange way beside me, covering her mouth and muttering something I could barely make out. By now, he had reached the highest branch of the tree.

"Two guavas...two guavas," she said, swallowing a fresh burst of giggles.

I looked up. My cheeks were on fire. Was it a fruit or a vegetable?

Up there, Manolito Ching's shorts were too short indeed.

twenty-four

Manolito Ching: neighbor.

Manolito Ching: friend.

Manolito Ching: crush.

Manolito Ching: interceding neighbor, friend, crush.

The nature of a thing (or person) is realized in the intent of its user. A week after Chi-chi's whisperings to the heir of the almost mansion, Tiyo Anding and my father were hired at the Chings' construction. Chi-chi and I did not discuss this happy consequence, but in my heart I wanted to apologize for thinking her easy, a flirt, grabbing at his arm like that and smiling her prettiest. She had a purpose, of course. She had more wit than I did, and she had mettle. Surely she had begged Manolito on behalf of our jobless fathers.

Mother was wrong. There is, in fact, dignity even in the abject state of begging. It takes great courage to beg and even greater courage to bear rejection. Ay, her lean heart, her fat spleen and my too young confusion. Which one to sweeten, which one to beg?

Supplication is a bitter business.

But I did not know that yet on those days of mooning over

the almost mansion. For a while, I stopped sighing at the window of our house from my bedroom. My eyes shifted across the road. Mother was wrong. There was something in her first-born that was worth a look after all, worth a hand on the arm. Surely a ball would dribble across the road again. I took to regularly pruning the hibiscus hedge on the front lawn, and VV joked that such industry could also hurt.

For a week, I couldn't climb the guava trees without blushing.

I erased stories: He did not slip ice into my dress.

I invented stories: He spoke for my father to his father.

In the kitchen where he saved me from fire-breathing dragons.

He snuffed out the fire with his kindness; he salved the spleen with it; he coaxed back the sweetness of the blood with it. In the kitchen, it should be the kitchen. It was the only part of his house where I could set my story. It was the only place where I was invited in.

His mother was there in her embroidered silk robe. Her face was heavily powdered, her eyebrows darkened into formidable arcs. Her most beautiful tortoiseshell comb with gold studs reflected the whirring of the fan, and she smelled of sandalwood soap. She was supervising the maid's cooking, rambling condiments, body parts and history, mixing them up, mixing up the maid's mixing. The blood stew was not going well at all.

"Vinegar curdled my husband's blood last year so we must mix the intestines with sugar, so business goes well with the mayor, and rub the pork shoulder with peppercorn, and get the garlic into the liver, then put more heart in his onion and sprigs of oregano on his spleen and don't forget to deepen his bile with green chilies, *entiende?*"

"Ay, no, ay, yes, Señora—I don't think we use spleen or bile at all, just shoulder and tripe and a bit of liver—"

"You teaching me how to cook my husband's favorite dish?"

"Ay, no Señora, of course not, *dispensa*—pardon me, Señora, but I'm not sure what to do anymore." The maid was wringing her hands before the ingredients of the master's order for dinner.

Dinuguan: "bloodied." It's pork blood stew with the vigor of offal. Black, sourish, thick and spicy, again with coconut milk. Truly a dish with character, literally with guts, and usually cooked for special occasions. But in the affluent household of the Chings, it was daily fare. Or perhaps it was cooked that night because the town mayor was coming to dinner. The two men shared certain favorites.

But spleen and bile? Talk about culinary surrealism. Each of us has enough spleen and bile as it is. Imagine if we fed ourselves with more.

"But the mayor is coming, don't you understand, you idiot? The dish must be complete, well rounded with everything close to his heart!"

The spleen is actually not too far from the heart, if we examine an anatomy book. Like the heart, the spleen is described as the size of a fist. Think of these organs as sisters, or perhaps one as the handmaid of the other. The heart pumps the blood, the spleen cleans it. Safe inside us, heart and spleen function in harmony. But out here where we often break one and vent the other, it's not easy to ensure harmony. Out here, there is little balance between our love and anger.

Mr. Alexander Ching loved his wife. Mrs. Soledad Ching loved her son. Manolito Ching hated his parents. No, that's too harsh. Dear Manoling was merely ashamed of his parents and hated to be seen with them. Perhaps he had appraised them the minute he was born and found them wanting. But surely he was kind.

The street gossips, who played cards at Tiya Miling's store every afternoon, often spoke of "that peculiar family."

"Ay, the boy never sits with his parents at church, if he comes at all. Now, if that doesn't tell you anything..."

"He prefers to live in the city, away from his folks, strange boy."

"Father busy getting richer and courting the mayor's favors, mother busy preening her jewels, all dressed to the nines, even at church. But the shoes, the shoes, just watch out for them—they're never a matching pair. Now if that doesn't tell you everything..."

"Father greedy, mother mad, poor boy. Locked in that mansion so scary with dragons and lions and all."

"But why build a mansion in our street—now that tells us nothing."

"Land is cheap among the poor."

"My street is not poor, speak for yourself!"

Gossip reeks with offal breath. Or perhaps with spleen in dysfunction, blood not quite cleaned. Bad blood, stewing blood.

"*Puñeta,* Gloria!" Señora Ching cursed the maid, who was now shaking before the beginnings of the blood stew that she would never taste. In the almost mansion, the dogs ate better than she did. The dogs had meat, regularly supplied by the local butcher. The servants had dried fish (their palates were supposedly less discerning) or whatever they could afford with the miserly pay. There were four maids and two drivers in a household of three.

"Didn't you hear me?" the señora continued. "I said spleen with sprigs of oregano and bile made greener by chilies, and the vinegar to soak that shoulder so the intestines can rest with peppercorns for the mayor's election next year. That's my husband's order, don't you understand, you idiot?"

Señora Ching was again mixing up the recipe, condiments mixed with history mixed with body parts. Shrill, pitched like a boiling kettle, her voice rose to the kitchen ceiling, then higher still, up to the red turret where she always locked herself for hours.

In his study, the señor heard her distress escalating, and came to the rescue. "Nerves," he murmured to himself, scratching his head in wonder, even if he had lived through scenes like this many times over. "The señora is just tired," he told the maid, then, "Come, my dear, you must rest."

Perhaps it was then that Manolito walked in, hands on his ears then on his nose, as he couldn't take tantrums or the scent of his mother's sandalwood soap, then he checked what was for dinner—

No, his hands were on his mother's arms, calming her with compliments in that soft voice of his, saying oh, what lovely soap, then he checked what was for dinner.

When he saw the assembly of internal organs on the kitchen table, he made a face. No, he sighed, smiling apologetically. He told his father he'd return to the city, that he'd leave before dinner, no, maybe after dinner, so he could escape his parents, no, so he could return to his schoolbooks.

The town's most powerful businessman shrugged, while the mother began to scream, "It's because of that dish, you know he hates it, it stinks like your mayor, and you never talk to your son, now he's leaving again, then he'll leave me forever and you don't even care!"

Mothers are wrong. Sometimes.

So he told her he cares, or did he?

That he'll never leave forever. Would he?

Certainly not. Surely he longed to dribble the ball across the road again.

And lest I forget, I'll end with a scene which, in my silly heart, I hoped happened as the blood stew boiled sweet-sourly, the offal gentled by the son's goodwill.

He spoke about two neighbors who could use a job at the construction. And the father acquiesced easily, kindly. You see, I always wanted to save the Chings from the spleen of street gossip. I always wanted to save Manolito, my first love that never went anywhere, from my own bad blood.

twenty-five

Perfumed heart tempura

You can never be sure about the destination of first love. Inside, it weaves its way to the core of that red fist lodged like a perpetual protest in the chest.

Be it rain or shine or rich or lean or sad or mad or glad, I'll tick.

Outside, the route is less definite. But the journey is as defiant.

Three days after I had overpruned the hibiscus hedge with my eyes set on the red gate, Señorita VV said I was getting "hyper" and needed some rest, so she'd prepare dinner herself, and could I go next door and pluck a heart.

I did not head straight to my old territory. I did a little restless tour of our street.

Towards the church, my eyes shifted between the red gate and the door of our house which I tried but abandoned, fearful that my mother would ask why I was gallivanting and I'd find myself staring at the white cucumber of her nape again, so I walked on, past the stone house where I caught a whiff of Mrs. Alano's burnt caramel, and then further, Tiya Viring munching her sweet tamarind and a book of romance, then

Juanito Guwapito arguing with his mother over the price of homemade peanut butter—all wrapped in life's exigencies. None could help me.

So I turned back, sighing at the volcano and the turret bisecting the sky, and wondering if one needed such power to win back a look, and hoping Nana Dora would know but she was busy packing up her pots, so I thought I'd ask Boy Hapon, probe his chickens' wisdom on romance, but that would be too daring, so I chose our door again but heard Mother's voice and lost my nerve. Thus, foolishly, I opted for the red gate where I could implore the dogs, the lions, the dragons to let out the boy with the ball.

But all I could do was stare at the iron lock, then cross the road again.

First love is too confusing.

What and where is the first route of the heart really? And how do we call it back after that restless wandering?

They say there is love at first sight between a mother and her firstborn. It is imperative for the child's survival. And there is love at first sight for the teacher who walks in on that first day of school with the smile of the sun, then kisses the bruised knee better. There is love at first sight for the boy or the girl who could smile like the sun and, just maybe, kiss better the daily bruises of growing up.

Falling in love. Throughout our adult lives, are we simply displacing that filial embrace with something that is like home, but as far away as possible from home's boring predetermination? Where the loving stroke of a hand is more of a genetic in-clination: Of course I love my own.

But how can I save that twelve-year-old from these argu-ments? Of course I love my own? Even today, it takes great ef-fort to believe myself.

To win back Mother, to coax back her blood and her knowledge that we share it. Whatever made her forget? That late afternoon, I nearly forgot that my chore was to pluck a heart, not to assuage it.

Pluck it and perfume it, then fluff it a bit with stiffly beaten egg-white batter, with a bit of salt to taste. First the banana heart has to be stripped to its palest core—where blood had been scared away? No, where blood is white and rich and sticky, and must be washed away. Because it is only flesh that matters, sliced thinly and dipped in the batter sprinkled with fragrant oregano, and deep-fried in sweet coconut oil till golden brown. And you serve it with spicy soy sauce.

Later that day, I realized that I need not have toured our street for relief. In my employer's kitchen, VV showed me how to make a heart unrecognizable from its own form. Not a fist now, but something more delicate, unthreatening, like little brown boats moored on a plate. But I could not draw true com-fort from them over dinner. They were not moored, but stranded like me who could never sail beyond my servile station.

In that lot of guavas and bananas, I knew my place.

After abandoning the red gate, I pursued my chore half-heartedly. Still, I played truant, choosing to climb the guava trees first, so I could save myself from my growing despondency. So I could feel the flush in the cheeks again. A face alive and tingling, like my hand fondling two unripe guavas. And I didn't feel ashamed; no one was looking. Then I applied myself to my assigned task. The banana trees flaunted their purple hearts, wantonly unfurling the outer skin here and there.

I could climb any tree in my time. I was a monkey. But I admit banana trees demanded that I be a very patient monkey. I kept slipping from the trunk, especially when my hand came close to the loot. I tried several trees. The hearts taunted me.

It was nearly six o'clock. I had been gone from my job for almost half an hour. My mistress, who never scolded me, would have much to say by now.

Then I heard it, the iron gate opening and the dogs going wild as a car drove out, just as I had wrung off a heart from its stem. On cue, I stretched my torso and neck, an impossible pose at that moment—dear Manoling in the chauffeured Mercedes smiling at me! I lost my footing and came crashing down, my skirt flying to my face and I couldn't cover my ragged knickers while holding on to the heart, of course, and God, it hurt.

How could I miss it? That smile breaking into laughter, loud and cruel, and a finger pointing at pale, pale me and my whitely bleeding heart.

twenty-six

Ginatan and curly hair

How many times can one fall from the sky? Is this the destination of first love, inevitably back to solid ground with a thump?

My parents, Gable and Marina: childhood sweethearts. Destiny: a one-room house plus a ceiling and six-going-on-seven children, and that inverse kinship between the heart and the spleen. The more one broke, the more the other vented itself.

As we progressed through summer, I went about my chores sighing long sighs. Worse, I found myself desperately tuned in to all the love stories of our street.

First, I noted a change in the *Lovingly Yours* program. Basilio Profundo's voice lost its deep timbre. The baritone stopped being a baritone, as if his voice had surfaced from the depth of a pool and was coming up for air and could not stop rising. Each day, his voice rose higher and higher, grating, metallic almost, as if edged with little knives. Ay, perhaps he was just being percussive, like his latest theme songs. You see, Patsy Cline's throne had been usurped by the Beatles. No more solitary heart-in-the-throat crooning. Bring on the drums, the tambourines, the electric guitars!

VV stopped tuning in to the program. Earlier she had told the radio man, gently of course, to stop offering his special *palitaw* every Sunday, then to stop visiting every Sunday, and finally to stop coming at all. You can never be sure about the destiny of first love.

Meanwhile at the other end of our street, Juanito Guwapito had other ideas. "Little Handsome Johnny." He was handsome indeed though a bit short (barely five feet), and all of aggressive eighteen. Tiya Miling's only son and the leader of the gang that drank at Tiya Viring's store each Friday night, just so he could spite his mother, had the most glorious blue-black curls. Exactly like the kind that saints and angels wore under their halos, if they had been as dark-haired as Filipinos. Mind you, our Juanito could have given them a run for their tall noses any day. His was perfect.

Looks aside, it worried me that he was my brother Junior's idol. The man had an oversupply of spunk and rah-rah-rah. He only drank *marka demonyo,* "mark of the devil," a gin so called because, though it had the image of the angel St. Michael defeating the devil, the latter wore a triumphant smirk.

Next to gin, Juanito Guwapito had always loved the Beatles, even before *Lovingly Yours* discovered them. At Tiya Viring's store, after too much *marka demonyo,* he sometimes practiced screaming like in "Mr. Moonlight" and "Shake, Baby, Shake," always causing her to beam with her usual amusement and tolerant graciousness. My brother Junior also took to straining his lungs and throat. It was some time before I recognized the source of his inspiration.

Juanito's curls were the kind that tickled your heart, even if you thought little of his other body or soul parts. Perhaps that was why he was always welcome at Tiya Viring's, or perhaps because his tongue was just as curly, a veritable tickler of hearts. That summer, he dropped by more often than usual at her store, even before Friday night, and always with a Beatles line that rivaled the sweetest snack in her jars. "I Want to Hold Your Hand," "From Me to You," "If I Fell in Love with You" and even "Help!" cried out with amorous conviction. Who could tell what conversations were exchanged between him and the woman twenty years his senior? Or if there were any conversations at all beyond his dropped sweet line. Under the for-rent comics strung like flags from her awning, he leaned towards the back cover of her Mills & Boon romance. "Go away," perhaps she had said, never allowing her eyes to stray from the page. But Juanito Guwapito had other ideas about the destination of first love. And how he fell.

Sometimes I wondered whether it was the Beatles or the nightly operas of Mr. Alano or the persuasive timbre of *Lovingly Yours,* or even her Mills & Boon that made Tiya Viring capitulate. And how she fell.

In that summer of broken hearts and vented spleens, this odd couple began their journey towards what should perhaps be our common destination: holding the balance between our love and anger. For when life overtakes love, isn't anger inevitable? It is easy to feel betrayed and even easier to upset the balance beyond repair.

But unlike my mother, Viring and Juanito understood

balance, the almost equal size of those organs shaped like a fist. Even many years later, they never lost track of their route. The heart pumped, the spleen cleaned, and the union most unlikely to succeed thrived, even if they were damned from the start.

My mother's union with my father was also damned from the start by her parents, but sadly she was not born to beam at the world from her book of romance. She wore her parents' spleen like a good daughter and I bore its weight also like a good daughter, even when I was still in her womb perhaps and sensing too soon that there would be no love at first sight between us.

But trust other loves to compensate for our lack and that no damning can derail them.

"How could that poor boy elope with a spinster old enough to be his mother? Ay, a most terrible, terrible scandal!" the card players were quick to declare when they heard of Juanito's fate. Meanwhile Tiya Miling howled to the half-moon.

When a star appears near a half-moon, the old folks say it's a sign that young couples are eloping.

"But *por Dios y por Santo,* she is not even young!"

That's why the star kept its distance and appeared at the other side instead, facing the half-moon. The star sat on the slope of the volcano, winking signals on that late night. And the half-moon rose from the dome of the church, like a yellow ear.

I remember that night well, because it was marked by the

bowl of very hot *ginatan* that I was trying to pass over the fence to my brother Nilo. It was one of those nights of my secret neighboring (after the mango disaster, I hid this occupation from my mother). I saw the lovers walk past about eleven in the evening. First Tiya Viring, seeming resolute with her small suitcase. Then, far behind, Juanito Guwapito with an overnight bag; he was in full stride, perhaps trying to catch up though she had begged that he keep his distance. Eyes fixed on their common destination, neither saw me. Well, I was hidden by the hibiscus hedge. They passed so close to me.

A diva's tremolo trailed behind, all the way from Mr. Alano's phonograph. Then all was silent again, as if the night were holding its breath.

Under the half-moon that spied like a yellow ear, Tiya Viring looked young, girlish. I had never seen her before in that frock of all the tropical fruit that you could ever wish for. She was at her festive, fruity best. And our curly-haired lover boy, ay, he was transformed. No adolescent cocksureness in those strides, just a purposeful dignity. Our Juanito Guwapito had suddenly grown up.

I froze on tiptoe, with the just heated bowl of *ginatan* raised like a chalice almost over the fence. On they walked, sure of their destination—towards the hidden garden of Boy Hapon. I thought of the chickens roosting on piles of Mills & Boon and his nightly reading, their appreciative crowing, and her daily reading—surely Boy Hapon had lent his chickens' love stories to Tiya Viring? And they said he had no friends.

"Hoy, Nining, give it to me—now!"

That did it. I swear Nilo startled the bowl as much as he did me. It teetered, then leapt from my hands. Sticky yam, sweet potatoes, sugar bananas, jackfruit and pearls of sago and, again, the proverbial coconut milk flavored with sweet anise scalded my poor brother's shoulder.

He dared not cry out, lest my mother heard. Again and again, he whimpered like a dying cat.

twenty-seven

Missing the Bicol Express

I knew I would never see Manolito again and would never want to see him again, even if I kept dreaming of his Beatles mop. And in my waking hours, I longed to go neighboring next door, properly that is, with a heaping plate to set in my mother's hands. But all I could do was ride on another love story. I was the angel destined to guard its secret.

I never told on the lovers hidden in Boy Hapon's forest of vegetables.

Yes, they had eloped to only a few doors from their own. No one saw them for a month. All believed they had run away to another town or perhaps the city. They reemerged only when both had rings on their fingers. Who knows how and where Boy Hapon arranged the wedding? Perhaps under a canopy of bittermelon, where the bride and groom each wore a crown of squash flowers and were bound in ceremony by a cord of legume tendrils, while the chickens crowed their joyous punctuations to a story better than any Mills & Boon romance.

Chickens are quite at home with good tidings. They greet each day for us in that hearty crow, whether the morning is sunny or wet. But human beings speak a different language, less generous and often the medium of spleen.

Where I come from, an old maid is an old maid is an old maid. And that means someone who has turned thirty. She "missed the last trip," she is a "frozen delight," she is a "chassis that's *kiribad*," bent and unusable.

"Ay, poor Juanito Guwapito, abducted by her who missed the last trip years and years ago too! *Santamaria,* what tragedy!" Our street was not wanting in unkindness. Tiya Miling was as damning as she was inconsolable. From the moment she woke up and found her son missing, then found out that Tiya Viring had not opened her store, she did not rest, putting two and two together in various combinations. The card players worked overtime.

"That evil woman—she had no right! When you miss the trip, you miss it! Ay, poor son, poor me!" Even years after the elopement, the offal breath still hung around the store of Tiya Miling. What spleen she had. Ever burning, fermented in a large harvest of chilies.

My town, in fact my region of Bicol, was known as the land of chilies, aside from being the land of coconut dishes. Other regions smirked about our women—chilies, hot. The men winked and sniggered. "Bicolanas are hot in bed!" I commiserate with these poor men. There, there, blame the chili for your unconsummated desires. And if it helps at all, take some crushed chilies to bed or wear them in your pants. Soothe that little aggravation there. My Señorita VV confided to me that she never had the courage to make such retorts when men from other regions made those insinuations at the hospital. Sometimes they told tales about how we secured our chili plants first, before we did our house, whenever there was a storm. Such was our laughable priority. We were a hot and trivial people. We even used chili not just as a condiment or spice, but as a main vegetable in the Bicol Express.

Why the dish was named after a train has always been debated. The most acceptable explanation is because when you eat it, your mouth burns so bad, you rush to the tap for relief, as fast as the Bicol Express! Quite prosaic a reason, an insipid match to the fire of the dish. This you cook with conviction, with courage. This is no dish for the weak at heart, I mean, mouth.

You begin with red and green long chilies halved, seeded, then soaked in water, so the usual bite is tamed. You slice these into short, diagonal strips. Then you cut into small cubes a handful of pork fat for an added wicked taste. Next, the coconut milk as always, garnished with chopped garlic and shrimp paste. Boil this with the pork till the mixture is thick and add the chilies. Then simmer until the coconut milk dries and leaves an oily base. A more than wicked dish for the heart.

Tiya Miling was hell-bent on exposing *her* wicked smile, *her* evil heart, *her* manipulative soul. The embittered mother spent hours with the card players, in a campaign against her daughter-in-law. She called Tiya Viring unrepeatable names, she spun tales about *that woman's* scheming or her family's scheming. Remember, Tiya Miling's heart was broken when her first beau married Tiya Viring's aunt instead, and that was just a small knot in these women's entangled histories.

Much later, I heard it was only after her first grandchild was born that Tiya Miling allowed Tiya Viring to step into her house, and she would not even speak to her. Worse, she humiliated her daughter-in-law, so her son packed up his new family from our street, from our town, and did not visit for three years. And through those lonesome years, with only the card players for company, Tiya Miling grieved and wondered, "Ay, where did I go wrong?"

For all our stories of sisterhood, there are women who will be cruel to other women and will lash out with the searing heat of chilies. And there are women who will remain unfazed by this cruelty, who will not run to the tap for relief, but who will deflect this heat with their own, beaming serenely, confident in their personal sun. I will always remember Tiya Viring beaming, munching and reading her borrowed romances, one ear to Mr. Alano's tragic divas or to a young man's dropped sweet line, tickling its way into her heart.

Years later, I was told that Tiya Viring and Juanito Guwapito loved and raised five children in a farm five towns away from ours. They planted rice, a forest of vegetables, bittermelon included. They also kept chickens and I presume piles and piles of Mills & Boon where they could roost. Surely they missed no train. It was the train that missed them, thank God, with its cargo of offal breath.

twenty-eight

Praying the *peccadillo*

Our street did not recover from the elopement. As if in sympathy, other affections began taking off to somewhere unreachable. "Mother stopped talking to Father and Aunt Rosario doesn't invite us anymore." Junior passed the news over the fence. "It's the fault of that thing in her tummy, ay, I'm going to torment it when it comes out, just you wait and see!"

Meanwhile Chi-chi and Bebet stopped coming around to see me. The twins disappeared from our street. I knocked at their door a few times, but no one answered. I watched out for their father at the construction, but I hardly saw him. He did get a job too, didn't he? Those were supposed to be happy days.

Manolito Ching also withdrew his rare appearances. The gossips suggested that he had absolutely refused to come home to the almost mansion. Even the Calcium Man stopped hawking. I found my sighs lengthening, as if they had no hope of ever concluding. I felt as if all our street had eloped from me.

But for many of the women, the worst desertion happened in the airwaves. *Lovingly Yours* was terminated, all passions gone kaput. Basilio Profundo had resigned, though the

summer wind was telling other versions of his program's de-
mise: the radio management could not bear Basilio's rising
voice, or his voice rose because he could not bear management's low pay, or because that girl sang "Crazy" and he lost
his mind then his voice, and switched to those screaming
mop-haired boys, so his fans protested and the management
was flooded with letters bearing less than love. So he was
sacked.

I imagined I was the only one who remained faithful. I still
longed to be my mother's best girl. I still cooked with the fervor to please or appease, perhaps in a sneaking wish to undo
the rice disaster and its hidden stories.

Even now, I know my passion will never be exhausted.

Passion can be exhausting, so I gathered when Señorita VV
began her fervent novenas to the Mother of Perpetual Succor.
Surely she was praying for poor Basilio's return, I thought. She
missed his floating faith, she had a change of heart. But soon I
realized that this fickle organ had veered towards another
direction. Patsy Cline was singing too regularly with Roy
Orbison in those Saturday jam sessions.

Peccadillos. Now where did I first hear that word? Ah, from
Dr. Valenzuela at the dinner table. He was talking again about
his American friend whose ex-wife loved *peccadillos*—"Ay,
poor Ralph, it would be good for him to travel, to get away
from it all," the doctor sighed. And Mrs. Valenzuela looked at
me, then frowned at him, as if to say I shouldn't be hearing
such things. Of course, I can hear them. I'm a cook and I
know *peccadillos* are fraught with risks.

The *peccadillo* is a dangerous fish dish. The *turingan,* a blue-grey fish, could be poisonous if not thoroughly cooked. It must be boiled in coconut milk with whole large green chilies, sliced tomatoes, crushed ginger, lemongrass if so desired, garlic and onion, and a bit of peppercorn. Make absolutely sure that the fish is cooked past danger, then simmer till the coconut milk dries a bit, as this is not a soup. Finally add some *pechay* leaves and season with salt.

Peccadillos. Only now do I understand this significant addition to my vocabulary that summer. As much as another addition: "the woman with loose molars."

You see, right after her loss, Tiya Miling began speaking in tongues, inventing fresh terminology for "that evil woman who stole my son." I must admit I was confused when I overheard something about teeth, as they shuffled cards.

"Please, what's a 'woman with loose molars'?" I asked my mistress.

Violeta Valenzuela could not answer. Her face was torn between laughter and guilt, neither of which I understood. *Loose morals.* She could not enlighten me about my confused consonants. She searched my face for any sign of accusation. She prayed more novenas. She even took me to church to pray with her, on occasion. Once as we knelt before the altar, she gripped my hand and cried out in a voice full of torment, "Ay, Nining, my heart is running away from me. Dear Mother of Perpetual Succor, help me catch it, please!"

How I wished I could make her feel better again. She began to lose her appetite and quickly lost weight. I applied myself to my cooking with even more ardor. Perhaps she would eat a little more tomorrow or the next day or the next, if I tried harder.

"Help me catch it, please!" If only the heart were a ball we could dribble and hurl anywhere or flippantly pass around, certain that it had enough rubber to bounce back into our breasts.

I tended my mistress with all the passion of my young heart, which I secretly hoped my mother would catch. Tomorrow. Soon. Even if I knew that it would always be hurled back not to my breast, but to these incapable hands, leaving them clumsy, criminal. I never did things right by her, I always let her down, I stole her dignity.

twenty-nine

Chicken barbecue: the way of all flesh

Just what would Mother say if she knew? What's a good girl to do after falling?

I burnt my ragged knickers.

My mistress asked why I was building a fire as I heaped dry coconut shells over the quickly disintegrating scrap of shame. I said I was making coal for the barbecue, which I had promised her yesterday, or had she forgotten.

She looked anguished, so I wondered whether she saw the thing catch fire, but why should that upset her? I ended up apologizing for the marinade. "Maybe I made it too salty, Señorita VV?"

She stared at me, no, she stared through me, at the fire that lit the early evening in the backyard.

Did she see that it was grey, like dirt, but it was not dirty, oh no, I washed it all the time. Mother said cleanliness is dignity and dignity is a must in our most intimate apparel.

I turned to my mistress again, arguing for the marinade. "I added beer and lots of garlic and chili, and even a bit of lemon, just as you like."

It was she who sighed.

Beside the soy marinade, the chicken legs looked white and sickly.

My ears perked up to all the noises of that evening, or perhaps for my mistress's next sigh. Then to the hushed voices from inside, her parents worrying about her, then the doctor talking again about the American who's arriving soon and perhaps he's getting over his tribulations, ay, poor Ralph, but such is life . . . and the cicadas began to hum.

Soon the coconut shells glowed. I fanned them. Tiny stars leapt up.

I had washed my knickers and mended them: the loose elastic, the fraying crotch. Then I hid them under my clothes, but only for a while. I kept seeing my skirt flying up to my face and my face would grow hot in bed. I kept seeing how he saw them: made from rough cotton sack used for sugar, and old. Then I heard him laugh in my dream and I couldn't breathe.

"Does . . . does your face ever grow hot?"

My mistress didn't hear. She was pouring the marinade on the chicken, kneading the meat. "I need to keep busy," she whispered to it.

"But you're always busy at the hospital, Señorita, and there's your college—"

"I mean, thinking is hard, so . . ." Her voice trailed away.

I thought about this for a while. We understood the same thing, we did! Thinking is hard, thinking is hard.

I took the chicken from her, I kneaded. Together we listened to the crackling fire. Then I said, "You'll like this, Señorita. It will be very good, I promise."

So much to say and ask that night. So much to think about. Inside me, words smoldered like the coconut coal ready for the meat. Thinking of him is hard. Thinking of Mother is hard. Thinking of him-Mother-him-Mother is harder. Thinking of falling is hardest. So I burnt my knickers. And promised to buy two nice pairs with my first pay. Maybe with pink embroidered flowers like my mistress's? And when Mother looks at me again, she'll see. She'll see.

Again, the sigh. "Do you like Mr. Alano?"

"He sings...uhmm...very well."

"Yes, he does, doesn't he?" she asked, as if unsure.

How the pale meat gasped as it landed on the barbecue, tightening into itself, then yielding to the fire, opening its pores, dripping its juices, then sizzling and slowly turning brown, gaining color.

Burning flesh is an undeniable smell. Burn, burn, burn.

I thought even harder. That insolent finger aimed at my shame, that cruel laughter rushing away in the chauffeured car. Of course, he was only hitting back because we saw. Two guavas, two guavas! I began to giggle, I couldn't help it.

"What's the matter, Nining?" For once, I had my mistress's full attention.

"The chicken." What was I to say? "It's...it's burning." Then I was laughing.

She frowned for a moment then began giggling too, as if she had caught up on a joke. "It's burning, it's burning, it's burning."

Quickly I turned the meat, trying to behave myself. "Better when slightly burnt, toasted, the outer skin, I mean. Crisp."

"Crisp," she giggled even more. Then, "Delicious magic," prodding the meat with a fork.

Magic, so she can find her appetite again?

"Try some, Señorita VV—you'll like it."

"I'll like it." She laughed, but strangely.

I was really lost by now, but couldn't say. I offered her a leg instead.

She held it close to her nose and sniffed it all around. "Will you come with me to the jam session tomorrow?" Then she offered me back the leg and left quickly.

Gladly I ripped the flesh off the bone. It was good, it was very good.

thirty

Leche flan, lechero!
(Milk cake, milkman!)

When Mr. Alano crooned "All I Have to Do Is Dream" through such incredible pipes, his band was convinced that among them breathed the one and only Filipino Roy Orbison.

And of course, his leading lady was equally a star.

It was a back-to-back show. Roy Orbison and Patsy Cline went through most of their popular repertoire. They even improvised, doing duets in perfect harmony, as if they shared only one set of lungs and vocal cords. It was the best jam session ever.

"When musicians start smiling, then the jam is gelling," Roy said. Then, cigar breath on the ready, he growled "Pretty Woman" too close to her ear and "Only the Lonely" inspired a gesture that brushed her shoulders. In turn, Patsy went all rosy and breathless through "I Fall to Pieces." I saw most of the action in close-up while eagerly awaiting Mrs. Alano's afternoon snacks.

Ay, yes, her confectionery sessions went on despite the upside-down epiphany on that fateful first Saturday. But she never came out of her kitchen again to listen to the three-hour performances and she wore cotton wool in her ears. I peeked and saw. Later I suspected that sour and bitter condiments began to stray into her mixing bowl. Perhaps she was trying out contrary tastes. An added pinch of salt here or drops of lemon there, and even an afterthought sprinkling of bitter nuts, gave a fresh nuance to her pies, muffins and cakes.

And what about her melt-on-the-tongue *leche flan,* a sweet dish with that exquisite texture between a mousse and a crème brûlée? This traditional flan had a slight bite from the burnt caramel, poured over it before serving. But this edge was no longer enough for Mrs. Alano. Suddenly tradition became too bland, like an excuse for a sweet, so she added grated lemon rind to her own mixture. And later, a touch of chili, not to burn, but to remind the palate that it cannot live on sweet whims alone.

Nowadays I sometimes speculate, perhaps erroneously, about the name of this dish: *leche flan,* a milk cake. But what about *lechero*? It's a swear word, which I often heard among grown-ups then. *Lechero ka*! Meaning, "You milkman!" Or what about, "You lecher!"

These speculations come from my memory of that afternoon when I was asked by my mistress to chaperone her. At snack time, it was Mr. Alano himself who served her the biggest slice of cake on a breakable plate with a design of red roses. The rest of us had only small helpings on plastic saucers. I saw how he came too close, as if the cake were meant to sit not on her hands, but on the front of her blouse. His hands accidentally slipped here and there, and his breathing grew funny, just as hers did. Then they disappeared from the room for some five minutes before the band reconvened.

Suddenly my cheeks grew hot and even other parts of me. I puffed air around, as one did to cool off. But I didn't know why I puffed more air into the front of my dress. I only knew I wanted more cake.

I couldn't sleep that night; it was too humid. Even the pictures in my head were sweating. They flashed as if in a peep show, in monochromes of red and always with two guavas dangling from a tree. I saw that I died and went to heaven, and God asked me what I wanted as a reward for being good. I shifted from one foot to the other, feeling too hot despite the perfect heavenly clime.

"C'mon, child, I don't have much time."

My eyes dropped to the flat front of my dress.

"Breasts for cake, Lord."

He scratched his head and thought deep thoughts. I realized He could not understand me. What did He know about cake? I was wrong about dreaming of feasts in the afterlife. Surely He ate rice gruel with fish sauce every day. As the priest said every Sunday, "God is our long-suffering Father." I felt contrite. It was not fair to bother Him with my silly ambitions, so I said goodbye and kissed His hands. Ay, I could not help but smile. Magic. In those holiest hands, I caught a whiff of our common poverty, pungent as fish sauce.

thirty-one

Hidden treasures: whitebait and candied sorrow

Magic. Making strange what is familiar. The most subversive human invention. Like cooking.

A week before I stirred serious magic in a pot, the Calcium Man was picking sour *iba* and Nana Dora was sweetening her sorrow. The *iba,* a green berry the size of a plump thumb, was face-crumpling sour. Her sorrow, the coconut that was picked too soon, was "no good, no good."

So I would later tell myself this story, in order to explain its consequence.

He wrapped the *iba* in *malubago* leaves. She grated the coconut and cooked it in palm sugar. Then he felt the sharp pain in his chest; it felled him for a few days, kept him tied to his bed, what a nuisance. She was exhausted, but there was much more to do for tomorrow's snacks. The candied coconut simmered, its sweetness steaming her face. He replenished his lamp with kerosene. She began to pound her sticky rice.

A young moon kept an eye on each of them, in their own huts a town away from each other.

By midnight, he was in a boat with the young fishermen who could have been his sons. They tolerated the old man who tagged along to pick the shells or seaweed that got caught in their nets. He always brought his own pail, a small net, more like a sieve really, and a little lamp. Tonight, he was "lighting" for *bolinao,* or whitebait, those finger-thin fishes that looked like a swirl of silver worms just below the surface of the water. He was slower than usual, but the other men did not notice; they were waiting for big game. With whitebait in season, big game came to feed.

She was falling asleep on her rice, her pestle always missing the mortar, but she kept on. This business of feeding, of assuaging hunger, was all-consuming. Her ten fingers made sure her customers were more than pleasured by her afternoon delights. Never mind if she had to prepare her ingredients till the wee hours of the morning. And she always cooked from scratch—nothing off-the-counter in her snacks.

For probably a hundredth time, he ruminated over his much-delayed stratagem. She sighed and refused to think. The young moon tried to pursue her thought and undo his delay. It disappeared from the sky earlier than usual. Day broke too soon.

I am speculating about the night before they finally caught up with each other under her hut. Magic. Because he unwrapped his sourness and she candied her sorrow.

Tomorrow, I'll see her, he'd promised himself, or the next day or—he never had the courage to time his meal with her arrival in the hut. But today was different. He set his lunch on her working table: steamed whitebait and *iba* berries wrapped in *malubago* leaves, and rice, of course. The *malubago* is a tree with yellow flowers, much like hibiscus. Its heart-shaped leaf is the perfect size for a fistful of whitebait and sliced *iba,* which, in its sourness, tempers the fishy taste. Steamed, the *malubago* leaf feels rough on the tongue. Slightly burnt, it gives the dish a quaint smoked taste. Sour, fishy, smoked: the palate is pushed and pulled by these impressions, inspiring ambivalence.

Face-crumpling sour or tongue-coating smoked, and even rough not just on the tongue but on all his vulnerable parts? How did it taste twenty years ago? How will it taste now should they meet again? He remembered her thoroughness, her meticulous hands that always smelled of some sweet thing. Again he pressed his chest.

Meanwhile in a JCM bus coasting a few streets away, Nana Dora sat uneasily with her three large baskets. She'd had this *kaba* in her gut since last night. Something might go wrong today, what with this thing curling and uncurling inside her like a restless animal. Again she lamented about her candied sorrow. Those pathetic coconuts! Too young, they ended up limp and watery in the palm sugar. *Aysus,* what measly filling for my cakes!

These cakes were my favorite of all of Nana Dora's snacks. A simple dish with no oil, no bothersome condiments. Just pounded rice filled with candied coconut and steamed in half a coconut shell. I remember how my first bite was always full of expectations, of a secret sure to be revealed, sweet and crunchy in that just-right way.

The JCM bus had never felt this stuffy, Nana Dora thought.

She opened the window behind her. Someone protested that her hairdo was getting seriously damaged, but Nana Dora shut her ears. So hard to make an honest living these days.

Under her hut, the Calcium Man could not breathe. Someone kept grabbing at his heart again and again. Ay, if I had sons, I would not be slaving in my twilight years. Such was his last thought before he slumped over his lunch.

This was how she found him.

thirty-two

Mung bean thick soup (and those that we can't see)

" 'I have grown old and feeble negotiating for my heart.' Believe me, Chi-chi, that was what he said when he came to at the hospital, and that was what caused the attack, well, I'm sure that was what he said, I was there, she asked me to come with the doctor—"

"Yes, the doctor," Chi-chi began, but I had more to say.

"He saved him, Chi-chi, rushed him to the hospital, I'm talking about the Calcium Man who—and you won't believe this—" Here my voice dropped a note lower, low enough for the listener to strain in attention. "Yes, the Calcium Man who is the husband of Nana Dora!"

"Is he in?"

"Now, isn't that the weirdest thing?"

"Nining, is the doctor in?"

Finally I caught up. "No—why—but he'll be back for lunch, come in, and whatever happened to you?" Finally I noticed the dark smudges under her eyes, like accents on a bad paint job. "Haven't seen you for a week."

She shook her head, then, "Mama collapsed, so Father can't go to work and we're all stuck at home."

"But I knocked at your door."

"It's very hard, Nining, it's very hard." She began to cry.

Disaster is worse on an empty stomach, so I sat her down at the table of the Valenzuelas, feeling like a culprit host. Yes, this is not my house, but this is my cooking. Suddenly I felt big and grown-up, like the richest patron of all the empty stomachs in the world. Come all ye that hunger into my opulent abode.

"Have plenty," I egged her, spooning more mung bean soup into her bowl. Then to lighten the air, I continued my story about the long-estranged couple and the origin of my soup (now this is even more incredible), shuttling from one tale to the other. "Stop, stop," she begged, "one at a time!" The tale or the food, what did she mean? Who cares? I dished out both with abandon.

"You know, my soup was made with the help of the ghost with big ears," I boasted.

This story grabbed her. She stopped crying, she even stopped chewing, but only for a while. "You really, really saw him?" she asked. Chi-chi would never have the courage to walk into Boy Hapon's kingdom.

" 'If you want, ask,' he once said, and I did. I have plenty of courage, you know," I boasted, feeling omnipotent, but I couldn't tell Chi-chi the full tale. That I knew Boy Hapon's secret, though I couldn't let on that I knew. He was just beginning to get neighborly with me. But I made sure my eyes wandered to every corner of his garden, seeking some sign of the eloped lovers.

He watched me for a while and said, "How to see through so much spleen in the air?" Then he gathered bittermelon leaves for my soup. I imagined he meant the spleen of Tiya Miling, so I wanted to say, but there's more than her wrath going around our street, and why don't you come out and find out for yourself? He couldn't, of course he couldn't lose his way in the thick of the spleen inhabiting our neighborhood.

Strange that what's meant to clean the blood creates bad blood, muddies it, and then we lose our way. So how to find our way through so much resentment? What to do to clear the air?

When I grew older, at each New Year, I always made the same resolution: to be a little less resentful. It's a hard one. As you try to reduce spleen for each day of the year, new cause for it arises; it operates like debit and credit. In the end, you find yourself with three hundred and sixty-five fresh entries in your account book. The air might even be thicker than before, so you can't see the heart of the matter.

Mung bean soup is so thick, you hardly see the bottom of the dish, but Chi-chi gorged and quickly saw it. I watched, my mouth echoing her mastication, tasting the magic of my green mung beans sautéed in garlic with dried shrimps and strips of pork, thickened with coconut milk, topped with bittermelon leaves and flavored with fish sauce. Then served to alleviate grief.

Her eyes had dried and were now going round and round as I concluded my tale. I told her about how Boy Hapon answered his own question.

How to see through so much spleen in the air?

"We need some purging around here," he said, looking up. His forest of vegetables could not obscure the cross and the smoking peak facing each other, blocked for a duel.

Boy Hapon had foretold what happened next. He had grown an angel's tongue.

thirty-three

Magic *igado*: with plenty of eggplants for purgation

We understood that the devil and the angel were equal partners in the balance of the universe. Their polar powers were duly recognized, whether it was with blame or with a benevolent heart. While we accused the devil of eating our words when we forgot something, we said "May you grow an angel's tongue" to reinforce someone's best wishes—may your words come true. Ay, I should have invoked the devil to eat Boy Hapon's words. But among his frowning fruit, I allowed his portent to take root. I kept quiet when he wished for purgation. I upset the balance of the universe by omission.

Or was it by commission?

Like when you commit to improving your immediate universe, but bungle the job. Magic malfunctioning. Magic missing a crucial ingredient: the real. For what use is magic if it's not grounded in reality, if it has no flesh-and-blood palate that you can manipulate into hope?

So I considered eggplants, plenty of eggplants. In my sleep, I conspired with them. They would not only aid digestion; they would purge the digestive faculties.

Then I consulted the whole neighborhood: Mrs. Soledad

Ching, Basilio Profundo, Tiya Miling, Nana Dora, Chi-chi and Bebet, the lot of them, even my mother. Well, not directly. Nightly I consulted their spleen. The size, the weight, the venting power.

Then I cooked it.

Igado is a liver dish, but spleen it was going to be instead. Nightly I made a pact with the butcher. He'd carve out the spleen for me in exchange for my perpetual patronage. If he wanted my soul, we could negotiate later.

I would serve spleen in a magic dish. *In my dreams.*

Feed it to the angry mouths of this world. *In my dreams.*

But my mother would eat the first meal. *In my dreams.*

And she would know how bitter it is. *In my dreams.*

And the bitterness would be unbearable. *In my dreams.*

But I would force it down her throat. *In my dreams.*

I would be both devil and angel. *In my dreams.*

And her stomach would heave in protest. *In my dreams.*

And she will be purged. *In my dreams.*

So cut the spleen into bite-sized pieces *in my dreams* then add diced sweet capsicum and hot peppers *in my dreams* and plenty of purgative eggplants *in my dreams* and onions and garlic *in my dreams* flavored by soy and the salt of her look *in my dreams* and the bit of sugar of her smile *in my dreams* long before she bore me *in my dreams* when she was still in love *in my dreams* with the young construction worker *in my dreams* whose tongue was never eaten by the devil only *in my dreams*—

The next day, the volcano erupted.

It had given no warning. It did not even rumble days before that fated lunchtime. After two tormenting hot weeks, when the humidity convinced us that we were surely taking a peek at hell, the earth shook, sending lunch spilling, rolling, falling from tables and running into each other on the floor of every household, as if the world were about to end in a sorry mush which we used to call food.

Then a loud explosion shattered the heavens before it rained ash for a whole week.

This was not in my dreams.

thirty-four

Pan graciosa: the bread of graciousness

"Another terrible stomach upset," my brother Junior said, un-fazed by the calamitous regurgitation. He understood that we lived on titled earth, that it could tip over any day but would surely recover its balance.

Everywhere, rice fields were reduced to mud from the lava flow, gardens turned grey or shriveled in even hotter air, food grew scarce and prices skyrocketed, and there was much hoarding of basic commodities. And the more affluent parts of the world visited us with their generosity, so I learned much later on. The "ghost" foreign aid, as we hardly saw it, flowed into our ports, and into the pockets of our politicians. Our town mayor suddenly became generous. Foreign aid was re-badged as "my personal aid" to ease the suffering of his peo-ple. On the side, he traded sacks of imported flour, powdered milk, sardines and corned beef on the black market. Much later, he would build his second mansion in Manila. "One eruption, one mansion." It almost became his epitaph when he died ten years later.

Summer in our street was usually endless blue skies with barely a cloud in sight. But that summer felt like a stifling prelude to a monsoon, a perpetual threat of rain that would never ever pour. The air was as dry as kindling.

Into this air, Tiyo Anding flew.

It was late afternoon. Mr. Ching had advised his construction workers to pack their tools and go home, and Tiyo Anding found it hard to breathe. There was ash in his lungs, his wife was extremely ill, his twins were hungry, there would be no pay that week and perhaps in the weeks to come. "No point in working under this damned ash!" Mr. Ching had said. Tiyo Anding sidled towards his workmates to borrow a bit of cash, but all were counting their last pesos.

A carpenter later retold that Chi-chi had come past earlier to ask her father for money to buy rice, but he had waved her away, swearing under his breath. No one thought much about that little incident until after the next day.

Tiyo Anding was the last to leave. First he packed his tools, then he walked around the fourth floor, which was thrice the size of his house. He studied the walls, he knocked at them: here lie the marks of my ten fingers. He stopped at each window and found that he could barely see the houses below. Everything was ash and ash and ash. Where was the volcano or the church, where was his left, where was his right? Was this his street?

He moved on to the next window. It was just a square on the wall, no glass or wooden frame yet. He ran a hand on the ledge. He made sure this was smooth, the measurements precise. He was a good mason, my father said.

It was a strong ledge. It was not hard to climb up and stand on it. It was not hard to step out and fly.

At the wake, the Chings were distinctly absent, including their maids. They could not bear to relive their shock. All four of them, including the two drivers, had to wash and scrub the driveway for hours. In her red turret, Soledad Ching did not stop screaming long after the body had fallen.

All were generous with donations. Mother sold her only jewelry, a necklace given to her by my father when they were courting, to buy the wood for the coffin which Father made. The Valenzuelas promised to assist with the medical needs of Tiya Asun. Mr. Alano offered his band for the funeral, for free. Mrs. Alano made cookies and muffins for the wake. Nana Dora cared for the orphans, cooking three full meals a day, from her own pocket. The Calcium Man, who was still in the hospital, donated his meager savings. Boy Hapon sent over vegetables that he had salvaged from his garden. The eloped lovers secretly communicated their condolences with an envelope of cash. Even Tiya Miling offered cases of Coca-Cola from her store and the card players paid for the flowers.

The Chings donated five hundred pesos and hired the funeral car, just before they shut themselves in their almost mansion throughout the wake and the funeral. Sadly there was no mass for the dead; the parish priest could not allow "such a death" to enter his church. Mr. Alano's band compensated for this ban. On the march to the cemetery, they played the religious hymns with great solemnity, as if the dead were an eminent personage. I swear heaven could have opened if not for the ash. It was extremely stubborn ash; it stuck. Surely we could not allow contamination beyond the pearly gates.

After the funeral, the afternoon snack was graced by freshly baked bread from the mayor's bakery, of all places. His was the most talked-about donation. It was a rare phenomenon indeed: the *pan graciosa,* the bread of graciousness. Hard white bread, one and a half hand spans in length and about five inches in width. It was the shape of a pillow, the shape of comfort. A comforted soul will be gracious, the mayor must have thought. Gracious and appreciative of the source of comfort, in next year's elections. He added cans of Star margarine and coffee though, just to be sure.

The bread of graciousness was filling bread; it seemed to rise even inside the stomach. It made at least eight slices, best eaten with a spread of margarine, then a good dunking in coffee. We loved the dunking. It softened the bread, which soaked up the merged coffee and margarine tastes. Post-dunking, the coffee left a fatty residue on the tongue.

My friends could hardly believe the grace that filled their table. Even in grief, they ate with relish. I saw them weep and eat and weep and eat.

becoming
a heart

thirty-five

Biko, a just-right sweetness

I remember looking up at shriveled grey hearts and wanting to dust them like a good housekeeper. The banana trees were not spared by the ash rain, and neither were the guavas. I looked up too much near the end of that summer, hoping to catch some color other than grey, perhaps a banana heart's purple or the chrome of the cross, the volcano's lilac. But all I kept seeing was a falling body, grey shirt, grey trousers and the greyest look encompassing the length of our street, also grey and indeterminate. From the air like that, it could have been any street.

For a while I feared it was my eyes that had turned grey and I had imposed the color even on my mother's face. Surely she had looked at me during Tiyo Anding's funeral, her face trembling, ashen. But I couldn't wipe it clean, afraid to also erase her eyes on me. So I looked down on the shovelfuls of earth instead, counting each thud on the coffin. So like my heartbeat. The earth was falling in here, in here, and I couldn't clean it up.

We were caught in a housekeeping frenzy after that eruption. Daily we walked around with a rag, a broom or a mop with obsessive industry, wiping off the residue of all fallen things. So when Ralph McKenna stepped off the JCM bus, he immediately believed we were a very clean people. Then he saw the standby boys stringing the *banderitas* from end to end of our street, criss-crossing them over our houses. He was delighted, he took photos of the multicolored bunting and had a Coca-Cola at Tiya Miling's, where he learned about the upcoming feast of our patron saint San Nicolas. He was overcome by admiration—a very clean and stoic people indeed. No eruption will stop their fiesta.

I marveled at the apparition that was soon knocking at the Valenzuelas' door. The American stood there, red hair protesting against the grey. Red as in red-red! I had never seen hair that color before, and we hardly saw any white men on our street anyway, except during eruptions when a few wandered around with awed, sweaty faces and cameras fixed on the volcano. But this white man was different. I was sure that his hair was the color of the stone that Father gave me: fire with the promise of burning. Of course, it had no black ridges or anything like that, but it would keep its promise at the end of that summer.

"Maraey na haepown," he said with a smile so crooked, I wanted to straighten it, to set it to rights. But I shook my head instead, hanging on to the doorknob, ready to shut it. Not that I was being rude, just slightly nervous. The giant, for he was a very large man, was deeply flushed and sweaty, as if he were drunk or painted with some moist blush-on. I had never seen serious sunburn before.

He repeated his greeting, for it was a greeting in our dialect

I realized later, his version of our "Good afternoon—*Marhay na hapon.*" But his attempt was lost on me and I could only shake my head. Then he tried something more complicated: "*Aetow haerowng* Dr. Valenzuela?" I nodded and shook my head again, understanding only my employer's name.

He laughed and shook his head too, as if to dislodge all that red on his crown, then finally reverted to his own tongue. "Good afternoon. Is this the house of Dr. Valenzuela?"

By that time, I had stepped back and instinctively pushed the door towards his face. His laughter had startled me; it was loud and echoey as if from a deep well in his chest. Then slowly I emerged from behind the door, with little confidence, so he shortened himself. He actually, well, almost, dropped to his knees, to engage me face-to-face. Then, voice a notch softer, he said, "I'm Ralph McKenna, a friend of Dr. Valenzuela," smiling sweetly, as only a crooked smile can be sweet.

So this is *the* Ralph. I felt my cheeks stretching. I was smiling back.

"You have a beautiful smile, miss."

My face grew hot, perhaps taking on a touch of the red silk on his brow. No one had ever called me "miss" before and none had ever, ever said I was beautiful. Or at least my smile was. Ralph, Ralph, my heart went.

"What's your name?" he asked.

I had no chance to answer. All I could do was note how green his eyes were, because the doctor, who had just arrived, was already raising the American to his feet, shaking both his hands vigorously as though he were about to pull them off.

"Hello, hello, welcome, Ralph, it's so good to see you. I can't believe this. How are you? How was the trip? Did you take the bus? Did someone drive you? Why didn't you visit earlier? Looks like you had too much sun—"

"Hold it, hold it, Andy," he said, laughing again from the well in his chest. "I'm very fine, thank you, and it's great to see you too. God, look at you, look at us now!"

They hugged, then continued talking, but Ralph did not forget me. "This girl has the most beautiful smile I've seen yet," he said.

I couldn't look at either of them, not without an acute sense of being caught savoring a stolen delight.

"Ah, this is our very dependable Nenita—Nining. Come, come in, Ralph."

"I like Nenita better." Ralph winked at me, before he allowed himself to be ushered into the house amid more questions and laughter.

I was left holding on to the doorknob, thinking, Nenita it must be from now on. As Ralph had said it, like a slow ascent and descent, gliding down on the *t,* softening it. Ne-ni-da. A name that would never sound angry, even when said in anger. I was used to my name being spat out at home.

"Some refreshment, please, Nining—and that nice *biko* you made yesterday, let's have some of that. Let's see how we can sweeten this American," Dr. Valenzuela teased, and the generous laughter bounced around the room again, amplifying itself in a bigger well.

Later I learned that Ralph McKenna and Dr. Valenzuela had

met in Oregon, when the doctor was an exchange student in a high school there. Ralph, now an engineer, came to work as a Peace Corps volunteer in a geothermal development. He had arrived in the Philippines two weeks ago and had been raving about the eruption. "I'm glad I caught it, God, it was incredible, Andy, I hardly slept, y'know, waiting for the fireworks each night, incredible, just incredible . . ."

The volcano talk followed me to the kitchen where I hurriedly warmed two slices of *biko,* a sticky rice cake cooked in coconut milk and palm sugar, with the slight flavor of *pandan* leaves. A simple snack, a just-right sweetness, not for sweetening Americans or any temper of any nationality for that matter. A just-right sweetness is only for recalling the memory of sweetness, its possibilities. Like when we wonder about a slight taste—what is it, where is it, how is it—and the wondering becomes more precious than the taste. It is the slightness, not the flavor, that is the gift.

Of course, at that time, I did not think this way. I simply believed that the essence of *pandan,* playing hide-and-seek in the palate, ensured my *biko* was not cloying, so a second helping was always possible. I added two more slices on the warming pan and hunted for some soft drinks in the refrigerator with little success. I came out to the lounge room with only the *biko,* and served my master and his guest on the best china of the house.

"Isn't your kid joining us?" Ralph asked.

An awkward pause, so I whispered, "We're out of Coca-Cola," my hand held out to my employer.

"Of course." Dr. Valenzuela quickly dug into his pocket.

"But I just had one, Andy—don't bother. Ne-ni-da, come, join us."

"Then have another, it will cool you down, you must be hot—here, Nining," the doctor said, handing me some coins.

"You have a lovely kid there."

"Oh, no—I told you my daughter's grown up, my only one."

"Niece?"

As I walked out the door, I heard the doctor say, "Maid," sounding apologetic. There was no rejoinder from the American, just a subtle clearing of the throat.

thirty-six

Sweet to very sweet

In the fiesta scheme of things, only the "can-afford" house-holds remained standing in dignity. Our house ceased to exist, because there was no bountiful spread on our table and certainly no sweetness. We were an embarrassment in a neighborhood especially proud of its desserts. How they trickled through our street, much like the sweetest rumors.

The Chings' *maja blanca,* a corn and milk-based, melt-on-the-tongue cake with strips of young coconut; *yemas,* syrup-glazed balls with a soft milky core; chilled upside-down cake with a fruit cocktail gelatin top and a moist chiffon cake base; *leche flan,* a rich and creamy eight-egg-yolk cake; the "stained glass" gelatin cake with all the cathedral colors shimmering in each slice—it's almost too beautiful to eat; *halo-halo,* the iced and milky "mix-mix" of candied fruit and jellies; *mazapan, buding, taldis,* all ground *pili* nuts fashioned into little cakes with the texture of slightly grainy chocolates; and sugar-coated *pili,* crunchy whole nuts slow-roasted in honey.

Tiya Miling's *buco* salad of strips of young coconut meat, pineapple, banana, *macapuno* balls, jackfruit, peeled grapes, raisins, cherries, diced apples and multicolored sago in sweet cream sprinkled with cheese; and *bibingka* made of grated cassava baked with coconut milk, melted butter, shredded young coconut meat, cheddar, topped with boiled egg yolk and strips of native white cheese.

Tiya Viring's purple yam delight cooked with sweetened coconut milk into a sticky, anise-flavored dessert topped with a thin spread of margarine.

Mrs. Alano's special *markasotes,* a hard cake baked from mostly egg whites and best eaten with freshly brewed coffee; her own version of *leche flan* with a hint of lemon rind and chili only for tough, enduring palates; and of course the definitive version of moist upside-down cake with imported almond slivers and glazed cherries, and a secret sprinkling of native bitter nuts for character.

The Valenzuelas' sweetened *kundol,* which is strips of *kundol* gourd slow-cooked in sweet syrup with whole *pili* nuts and flavored with the tangy *limonsito* berries; and the fiesta *biko* with strips of jackfruit and a generous topping of palm sugar plus slivers of young coconut meat, all cooked of course by my own hands.

Ay, so much sweetness trickled through our street and ran us down. In that grey season that tried its best to be festive, we shrank away in our shameful inadequacy. Junior even intimated that at home we were slipping into the rice gruel and fish sauce routine, as Father's job at the Chings' construction was taking too long to resume. But thank God, Mother did not lose her dignity for too long. I was paid my first monthly wage. And thank the saints, my siblings' little tummies were reinstated on the map. Señorita VV made sure we had a share of their feast, every dish of it, down to dessert. The Valenzuelas' sweetness trickled through our street indeed, but not to run us down. It defied walls in the spirit of generosity. It went neighboring. And with tales that ranged from the sweet to the sweet-sour to the unsweet, but never bland.

Let's begin with the sweet *kundol,* my own creation. Its fate simmered in quite strange circumstances during the eve of the fiesta, which trickled from the sweet to the very sweet, concluding in the town dance, where the American learned about our gradations of sweetness.

Limonsito berries. These diminutive, crimson berries make the dish, more than the *kundol* gourd. They have a clear, sticky juice, like colorless nail polish. The twins and I sometimes used them as such, when we got bored, flavoring our nails. Slightly sweet, slightly bitter, slightly burning—I can scour every corner of my tongue and not quite find the words to do justice to this quaint taste. All I know is it reins in the sweetness, remaining coy, playing hide-and-seek in the palate: where is it, what is it, how is it?

Ralph must have asked that question when he first saw my mistress, as she was breaking a crimson berry between her teeth. She had just woken up from her siesta and was wearing a white shirt that reached only to her bare upper thighs. Her hair was loose and as agitated as her face, she was close to tears, telling me that she'd stop singing for Mr. Alano and she wouldn't sing tonight, definitely not, and I answered, but you're wonderful, really, and the dance won't be a dance without Patsy Cline, while feeling helpless with my hands full of strips of soaked *kundol*—then Ralph walked into the kitchen.

His smile was even more crooked as he stood there, gazing at her.

I looked at him, I looked at her. His face was turning redder by the minute, even his ears.

"You must be Violeta, Andy's daughter. Hello," he said, coming closer and extending his hand. "I'm Ralph, Ralph McKenna."

My hands wrung out the water from the *kundol* strips with too much enthusiasm. Ralph was wearing an orange shirt and a woody, herby scent that made me want to keep inhaling, ay, what is it, how is it?

Señorita VV pulled her shirt lower and took the proffered hand, embarrassed about her disheveled appearance, but only for a while. "So you're the Ralph—hello," was all she said and left us. I saw that he went on looking at the door long after she had gone.

"I think I need some water." He was smelling his hand, stained with the sticky juice of the berry. He didn't say my name in the usual way. He didn't say my name at all.

Later in the day, I went neighboring next door, my first attempt since the green mango disaster. I took home my first full wage, all of twenty pesos, and the sweet *kundol* and various savory dishes, and some clothes for the night. Mrs. Valenzuela said I should visit my family, perhaps sleep at home, because it was the eve of the San Nicolas fiesta. I should be with family, at least for tonight. So I cleaned the house and the garden, and cooked most of the feast for the next day.

Meanwhile Ralph hovered around, making conversation with my employers, sometimes staring at Señorita VV's bedroom door. "We're worried about her, Ralph, she's been acting strangely for weeks. She locks herself in there when she's not at the hospital or at her college. I hope she doesn't forget she's singing for tonight's dance."

"And she sings too?" Ralph sounded more wistful than impressed.

"Lucky you, Ralph, you don't have children to worry about. Look at me with all my grey hair, and yours still as red and thick like when we were back in Oregon. So was it an amicable divorce?"

Ralph sighed.

Some sweet is always tucked into a sigh. I seek it, even now. I shred the tiny exhalation, be it elated or mournful, believing it is hiding there.

My father sighed, my siblings sighed, my mother almost sighed when I laid my offerings on our dinner table. It did not look as rich as the table at Tiyo Anding's wake, but in our house this spread of dishes was alien, especially with the twenty pesos, which I had laid out as well. Each crisp bill was a punctuation of abundance.

"Pride," Mother said through her teeth.

"But, Maring..." Father chided her with a funny croak in his voice.

Then Junior called out, "We'll also have a fiesta!" to my mother's back disappearing into the ceiling. His bravado prompted me to add, "And I'm sleeping here tonight, isn't that great?"

She stopped in mid-ascent. "But your siblings have been sleeping comfortably with more room."

From where I stood, I could not see all of her. It was like being denied by only half of her body, from the womb to her feet.

"Maring, how could you?" Father said, running after her.

My siblings stopped in their tracks, suddenly unsure. "Sit down," I said, in a tone more grim than inviting, and brought out five saucers and teaspoons from the cupboard. "This will just be a tasting, get me? The fiesta is tomorrow."

Quickly they came back to life, grabbing their share, a teaspoon of each of the savories: the goat meat *calderetta* with its sweetish-sour sauce, the pork and chicken *adobo,* the *mechado* with its little *mecha* or "wick" of fat peeking from each chunk of pork, and the beef *afritada,* all steaming in their oily paper plates. It was one of those rare moments when our house smelled rich. The hearty aroma of meat floated in and out of garlic, hot peppers, parsley, bay leaf, green onions and sweet capsicum.

"Hoy, I said no more than a taste!" I silenced protests, slapped greedy hands and righted long faces, but with little success, because sometimes only a taste can be more distressing than pleasurable, a very miserly treat. Like endearments in half sentences or embraces not coming full circle, ensuring the torment of gaps. I thought of the boy who touched my arm, only my arm...

"And the sweet *kundol*?" Nilo asked, licking his saucer. He had devoured his share too quickly.

"After everyone finishes, okay? And again, only one teaspoon each."

"You're rich!" Junior said, hiding one of the pesos behind him.

"I saw that, put it back."

"Just one, Nining," he said.

"Me too." Claro also grabbed a bill for himself, and everyone did the same, even little Elvis.

"Hoy, don't be greedy! Hand them back, quick, or you won't get any sweet."

Reluctantly, each one behaved, including me. I'm grown up now, I thought. I need not appease my own hunger for sweetness. After I handed all the twenty pesos to my father, I left the house, my clothes for the night tucked under my arm. Mother was right. My siblings needed more room.

Outside, the grey pall was not visible at all. The whole street was awash with light and Mr. Alano's band was in the middle of "Pretty Woman," in the vacant lot beside Nana Dora's hut. I crossed over to the site of the town dance.

The few banana trees had been cut down for more space, and bunting and multicolored lights were strung over and around the fenced-in crowd, all freshly showered and in their best attire, smelling of "spray net" and cheap cologne. The women's hair was stiff and teased up, the men's generously pomaded. There was a nervous thrill in the air between them, seated on opposite ends of the dance space, modestly checking each other out, hearts covetous and anxious all at once. What if she says no? What if I become a wallflower? What if my hands sweat?

When I grow up, I'll never go to a dance, I promised myself. I'll die of covetousness, I'll shrivel against the wall, and my hands will keep sweating even in the afterlife.

I crouched against a banana stump among the shadows, watching the town dance, called the *kudal-kudal,* the "fence-fence"—a woman could be "fenced in" by an ardent suitor who would expect her to dance only with him throughout the night. And the dance that mattered most was "the sweet," or if you were lucky, "the very sweet."

Ma-sweet na, ma-sweet na—it's about to be sweet, about to be sweet!

When the first strains of slow music began, arms tingled in anticipation of the sweet, or the slow-drag, in our street where the watchful cross strictly banned the body's wayward desires. The dance floor was the only legitimate place to hold someone close, but not too close. If a woman danced very sweet, she was considered loose, easy.

The band meandered through its introductions, slow and easy. The men shuffled across to the women, hands extended. My Señorita VV picked up the microphone as Mr. Alano nodded to her. She nodded back, breathed in, then belted out "I Can't Stop Loving You" in true Patsy Cline style.

It was not until the fifth sweet that I noticed the red-haired giant leaning against the fence outside, eyes only on the vocalist gleaming from her swept-up hair to the sequins on her pink shoes.

thirty-seven

The flight of tails
(With eggplant and banana heart in peanut sauce)

In the wee hours of the morning, I listened to Boy Hapon's chickens, their exclamatory footnotes on romance. I could not sleep. I could have been sleeping at home. I thought of Mother, of how miserable she looked. After the baby is born, she will be sweet, she will be sweet.

Thou shall not covet thy mother's sweetness.

So I thought of Patsy Cline instead, storming off after an argument with Roy Orbison, and the radio man suddenly resurrected from the wings, trying to walk her home, and the American watching from a polite distance, perhaps biding his time to offer the same ambulatory assistance.

But I was the one who walked her home, explaining, "I'll have to sleep at your place, Señorita VV, you might have early guests tomorrow, who knows," but she was not listening. She was walking too fast, her sequined high heels clip-clopping on the pavement. I felt rebuffed for the second time that night, but her tent dress softly brushed my arm with each step and I felt comforted. "You were very good, you know," I ended.

The next day was too busy for despair. Even my señorita

was up and about, entertaining friends from her college and the hospital. There was a steady stream of visitors, thus several breakfasts from seven till ten and at least four lunches till two. I was cooking, serving and washing up nonstop, with two other maids hired for the day. Outside I could hear the fiesta band, not Mr. Alano's though, playing the usual marches from house to house.

A fiesta is a gustatory tour. It is a lesson in eating your fill through strategic moderation. You do not feast in only one house, but tour the tables of the whole street, sometimes eating multiple breakfasts, lunches and dinners, and taking home wrapped portions of the feast, forced on you by generous hosts. Best to have only a modest helping in every house, or perhaps just the best dishes, in order to accommodate everyone's generosity. And space these feastings, making sure your stomach settles down after a meal in one house before you proceed to the next. Be very mindful of unspoken rule one: You must never skip a friend's or a relative's house, otherwise there will be many hurt feelings and recriminations.

And unspoken rule two, for the host this time: You *must* have a fiesta! An empty table is shameful, even criminal. It kills your *amor propio,* your self-respect. Your house disappears from the map. So you turn your pockets inside out and if they yield nothing, you borrow fiesta money, perhaps for one or two dishes lest a guest drops by. Never mind if you beg the kindness of usurers and shrink before their eyes. You put your self-respect on the line, in order to keep it on your guest's full stomach.

Finally, unspoken rule three: You do not go feasting in your own feast. You are the host, not the guest. Not for the twins Chi-chi and Bebet though, who chucked out all the rules long ago, as easily as they did bones or corncobs gnawed bare and thin. They reinstated their stomachs on the map. They went feasting on our street's collective heartbreak that summer—their father forever flying in our eyes.

As I spooned each dish onto the plates of my employers' guests, I imagined Tiyo Anding flying, with his long, long esophagus trailing behind like a tail, but he did not slam against the driveway of the Chings. He only kissed it—a tail-kiss, a genuflection, then he took off again. Then Tiya Asun followed, tail as distended, then Chi-chi, then Bebet, their eyes going round and round in unison. They flew over our fiesta, floated in and out of the grey, feasting on the aroma rising from our kitchens, tables and bodies hell-bent over plates, certain that this posture will ground us, this act of keeping the esophagus in its right length.

Their tails lashed about, their tongues flooded, and they gulped the fiesta air, filling their lungs with—

Boy Hapon's fish roe with bittermelon and his secret
    ancestry
Señora Ching's roast pig wondering about her son
Mr. Ching's blood stew currying favors from the mayor
Señorita VV's pork *mechado* languishing on her plate
Ralph's *adobo* stirring him with bay-leaf longings
My beef *afritada* accusing my father's silent mouth

My chicken *relleno* turning bitter on my mother's tongue
Mr. Alano's *paella* made richer by his quandaries
Mrs. Alano's *embutido,* her pork roll with pickled endings
Tiya Viring's and Juanito's eloped soupy *pochero*
Tiya Miling's offal burning in hot peppers and sorrow

We are touring my street again, reliving this flight of tails, which concluded in Nana Dora's hut. She was there with her pots, refusing to feel redundant in a street where, for a day, every dish must be home prepared. She looked up and cringed at the flying tails. She waved her carving knife at them, demanding that they land, now! She threatened to chop off the vision—because hunger is always unsightly. It's our gut hanging out, unkempt like unassuaged love. We see it in someone else and instinctively we grab at our own stomachs, then quickly withdraw our hands, knowing we have betrayed ourselves.

But Nana Dora was forgiving. She did not cut off their tails; she ransomed them. She chopped the oxtail in her pot instead, for she had come prepared, and cooked it with a shriveled banana heart, a casualty from the site of the town dance. A tail for a tail, with a heart thrown in, and the cloves of crushed garlic, the tear-inducing onions, the eggplants, string beans and toasted rice simmered in peanut sauce, which turned a touch vermilion with the *achuete* spice—and she served this ransom to her guests, just landed and catching their breaths, with sautéed shrimp paste.

She almost believed their tails would behave and restore

themselves to their old place, respectably hidden again like her own hunger. But tails are beyond ransom; they know it is common hunger that makes them family. The family of the deceased was grateful for Nana Dora's attempt at assuagement. They delighted in her repast, for was this not about her feeding as much as theirs? Then they took off again, tails linked together, making a scallop pattern in the sky. Off they flew to where the sun set behind the volcano, and disappeared forever. I missed them, I missed them.

thirty-eight

Tiling-tiling's ice drop

When Chi-chi said goodbye, she recounted with relish how they had feasted on Nana Dora's *kare-kare*, the oxtail stew, under her hut. My affection for our prickly chef of snacks grew—so three weeks after the funeral, she was still caring for the orphans, or perhaps giving them her own taste of farewell, soupy and savory. Tiya Asun's family had decided to leave our street for her village fifty miles away, for good. "Ay, tell me now, Nana Dora, how can I live with this? A few paces from my house is *that* window, and it will always be there, always. Ay, how do I live with this?"

So I concocted my own recipe for farewell. I borrowed five pesos from Señorita VV and begged for an afternoon off with my friends and siblings, then I prepared our old haunt. Under the gaunt banana trees and their browning hearts, under the guava trees that would refuse to flower until after a year later, I watered the dried-up earth. Here, we did girl things together, like curling each other's hair with cassava tendrils and painting our nails with *limonsito* berries, and our lips with the crimson flowers of *oro-alas-dose,* then mincing around in make-believe high heels, which meant a stone tucked between heel and slipper. Then we fried dead beetles in hibiscus leaf oil and made mud cakes on the side. Then, all done up like high society misses, we squatted around this pretend meal, spooning the beetles and mud close to our mouths while smacking our lips and telling stories about food, real and wished-for: hoy, what will you eat when you grow up?

When we grow up, our stomachs will have grown too, and our mouths, and our capacity to make them happy. During those afternoons of wishful play, we never doubted this, that happiness was simply gustatory and sorrow meant gruel and fish sauce for the rest of our lives.

I would never see my friends again. They would die before they turned twenty. I would always remember them in that afternoon before they flew off, tails linked together, to where the sun set behind the volcano.

Any minute now and they would be here. I burrowed my toes into the drenched earth, feeling more than hopeful. I was set on my own fiesta; I was the host. I looked at the five pesos in my hand and did my sums, then went off to buy ten Labyus, two bags of *galletas patatas* and three packets of Fat & Thin from Tiya Miling's, then waited under the guava trees.

One by one, my siblings slipped out of our house and joined me, even Junior, whose main object was the free snack and the possibility of *tiling-tiling*'s ice drop, which would come much later. Junior didn't like the twins. "Too girlie, too hungry," he used to chant, as if he were above hunger. I noticed that since I left home, he had grown surly and he took more risks with my mother. He answered her back, Lydia had told me, or rather, mouthed the answer behind her back, if he was not shaking a fist at her, also behind her back. He had become a wicked little man with the habit of squinting and biting his upper lip.

I watched my siblings troop towards me, their bodies not quite certain at first, still half-angled towards our house, waiting to be recalled. Lydia's hair now reached the small of her back and Nilo had grown an inch taller. Claro was learning how to manage his snot and Elvis could say his full name, Elvis Rodriguez, without eating the last syllable. Quickly they spotted the feast stacked on a crook of a guava tree, and advanced with more purpose, grinning as if their faces would split like little pods.

I could not tell what it was, but there was a strangeness about them, well, with me. A kind of awe. They gaped and smiled with pleasure, the way they did at the last morsel on a plate. "You fat," Lydia said, pinching my cheeks and giggling. I must have filled out, I must have grown too. "Fat," Elvis echoed, also claiming my cheeks. I hid my face on his little shoulder, feeling as though I had a cold.

"Okay," I clapped my hands, playing the eldest in control again. "We're having a party for Chi-chi and Bebet, because they're going away."

"You don't even have Coca-Cola. How can you have a party?" Junior snorted, biting his upper lip.

"Hoy, don't be mean."

"Why are you feeding those girls? You should just feed us."

"You greedy little thing."

"And you rich and all that."

"I'm not!"

"And it's your fault!"

"What?"

"Nothing..." He released his lip, then turned away.

Nilo sneaked behind him and pulled up his shirt. I saw welts. "Junior!" I cried, rushing to him.

"Aw, don't be such a girl!" he grumbled, brushing off my hand.

It was then that the twins arrived, shuffling their feet. Their faces hung to their chests and they held hands as if anytime they'd flee and be done with it. I felt I'd made a big blunder, forcing them to face up to a loss. Farewells are soupy, yes, or moist, like when you have a cold.

I wanted it so much to be right that afternoon, yet we had grown suddenly awkward, even tense, with Junior getting more surly by the minute. I opened my packets to save the moment. Shortly, Lab-yus melted on tongues and lips turned white with the very salty melon seeds and the crisp *galletas patatas* crackled in the air, and some spirit was restored. Then, as if to complete the restoration, the *tiling-tiling* rang from a distance, and ears perked up, and I said, "Yes!"

Everyone rushed to the approaching ice cream vendor, the *tiling-tiling,* the bell. It tinkled, it teased, telling us how hot it was and how lovely to cool our throats and tongues with an ice-cream cone or an ice drop. All preferred the latter, a milky ice bar molded with strips of coconut meat and a sprinkling of cheese and raisins, so I used up the last of my borrowed money. Shortly we were squatting under the trees, fervently sucking our ice drops, our tongues growing slightly numb, our throats cooling, and we thought of monsoon and rivulets of rain between our toes, even as steam rose and rose from the earth. The moistness quickly disappeared.

Then, I don't know why, I said, "If you always leave rice in the pot, even a single grain, then there'll always be something to eat in the house." I had broken the spell. Chi-chi was frowning at her ice drop, as if there she had read her retort: "But what if there's nothing to leave, Nining?"

I had blurted out a folk saying, my going-away advice, which sounded more like insult added to injury. I didn't answer her, just kept my mouth around the ice drop, freezing my tongue.

"But you must always scrub the pot clean, Mother says." Nilo there, being literal.

We nibbled at the strips of young coconut, we found the cheese and raisins with our tongues, we sucked the thinning ice bars, we swallowed conversations. I could hear our concerted slurps of pleasure. We squatted together for the last time, thoroughly occupied, until nothing was left in our hands but a stick licked clean.

"You're really leaving?" I asked.

"Leave us in the pot," Bebet murmured.

"Yes, in the pot," her twin echoed.

thirty-nine

Coconut *kalunggay* blues: "O come home, Tasyo, come home"

Nana Dora said going away is like leaving the table after a meal. You go away, because you have had your fill. It would be too greedy to stay on. I wondered whether she meant my friends were greedy.

"Say, in a fiesta, after the main dish maybe you go, even before dessert, because maybe the host doesn't have any, you understand?" she asked, searching my face.

I hated her strange speech in that soft voice. It added weight to the heaviness in my chest. I wished she'd be her prickly self again. I kept trimming the hibiscus hedge, but I didn't look across the road anymore.

Each cooking day, after Nana Dora had packed up her hut in two baskets, she caught the first JCM bus that came along. But today she had ambled towards the Valenzuelas' instead, as if she were just passing by or dropping off some anecdotes about eating and "these people." How could she talk about my friends, the orphans that she cared for, as though they were strangers?

She set her baskets down and began fanning herself. "Too hot, too hot—now, Nining, maybe you should know these people a little bit more—here," she thumped her stomach. "Then here," she thumped her heart next, "here would be lighter for you."

A hibiscus blossom fell at her feet, then another, but I didn't care. I kept snipping leaves and flowers alike, intent on shaping the hedge.

She began fanning me. "And why should you call them back to the table anyway? The meal is finished," she said, her eyes wandering across the road to the Chings' construction, up to the fourth floor, then looking away. She fell silent. She fanned herself then me, then her again, as if willing the air to make conversation.

How can I call them back, Nana Dora? I don't know where their village is, fifty miles away. This morning, I went to ask them how far is fifty miles, but their house was empty. The door was open, as if they would return any minute, so I went in, but it was dark and smelled of sickness, and they won't come back for that, will they?

Nana Dora helped me to clean up the fallen leaves and flowers. "If, say, the husband leaves the house soon after a quarrel, the wife should hang his shirt over the stove and whip it several times, that way the husband is certain to come back. If he doesn't, she must sing while she cooks, 'Come home, Tasyo, come home!' Then if she sits down to her first meal without him and she chokes, he's remembering her from far away. Not that he's coming back, really..."

I stared at her. The fan was still, she was holding it close to her chest. "What, Nana Dora?" She had confused me with the folk beliefs that seemed to have afflicted her tongue. "Tiyo Anding didn't quarrel with Tiya Asun . . . and he's not coming back."

"The meal is over, that's all," she said, and flagged down the JCM bus that had appeared around the corner. "And there's no dessert," she added, picking up her bags and boarding the bus.

How could I know that Nana Dora was commiserating with me in her awkward way, with her own story of departure? I was twelve years old, literal and preoccupied with my own loss; I even forgot to ask about her Calcium Man. But before that summer ended, I would find out more about the man who was still negotiating for his heart with the estranged wife whom he had abandoned twenty years ago. Because her womb was as barren as soup without water and he so badly wanted to have sons. Three years after he walked out the door, though, Anastasio "Tasyo" Guerrero did come home, but her door was closed by then to his claims of love and regret. No dessert, the meal was over.

A year of whipping his shirt by the stove, another of singing before her cooking, and all along feeling as if her solitary meals were not chewed enough, that they clogged her throat and were always too painful to swallow. Then in the third year, she threw all his shirts away, stopped singing, grew prickly, but she never choked on her meals again. She perfected the art of eating alone. Then she grew into the habit of cooking herself little treats every afternoon after her siesta, dishes that heightened their flavors at each meal, blessing her tongue. Her *turon* became crispier, sweeter, her *biniribid* more sticky and succulent, her rice cake with candied coconut stuffing more delicate, and all her native concoctions became too good to keep to her plate alone. So she sent them neighboring—a plate of coconut-smothered *palitaw* for the kids across the road or a bowl of gingery-sweet *ginatan* to the old seamstress next door. Soon her neighbors longed for a regular helping from her kitchen, so they urged her to open a small business of snacks in her town. The business thrived, but with a regular irritation that made her grow prickly as each day passed. Tasyo kept "coming home," on the pretext of buying a snack. She always refused to sell him any: you'll never taste the labor of these hands again. Soon they both grew old and tired of the drudgery of coming home and refusal—what predictable rhythm. She moved her business to our town, our street, and years later he followed her, daily hawking his own wares, but never found the courage to plead with her again.

I did plead, then I purged (in my dreams at least), but with little success at home. So how to know when to stop? I never had the conviction of Nana Dora.

"O come home, Tasyo, come home!" she pleaded over her *kalunggay* in coconut milk. Her song took on the rhythm of her grating coconut, of her squeezing it for milk, pressing harder when she sang the last syllable of her husband's name, as if this too could be squeezed for its withheld affection. The pleading-wishing ritual humbled her, but never mind. She stirred the milk in her wok, with shrimp paste and dried fish heads, garlic and chili, while singing "O come home" in different keys.

Perhaps a wish needs to be tested in different keys. This allows us to test out the act of wishing in our mouth, our ears. Thus we are able to check ourselves, certain one moment, ambivalent the next: how does this taste, how do I sound, is this what I want, and how desperately so?

Then when the milk simmered, she added the *kalunggay* leaves and her stirring stopped; so did her wishing. She must not stir the leaves at this point or else the dish would grow bitter. She must not persist with her pleas, otherwise she might turn out as bitter. Humility is only a stone's throw away from humiliation.

But not in other households. For years, Señora Ching pleaded in her red turret, which never opened again after a body flew down to the driveway. The Chings closed their books on that tragedy and bought the flying man's house, so their construction could breathe and expand. But the señora found that breathing made her weary as she hung her heart on the red gate, hoping for her son's return. "O come home, Manoling, come home!"

It echoed in my breast, sometimes.

Manolito Ching had decided to live in the city. Later he moved to Manila, away from his mother's madness and his father's affiliations with the corrupt mayor. The señora's wish could not bring him back, because it never ventured beyond her turret, remaining constant and contained.

It was different for Tiya Miling. Yes, she too hung her heart on the door and in her offal breath chanted her own longing, but this was bearable. It was not constant; it was made impure by anger. It ebbed and flowed with her son's favorite Beatles songs, played on a brand-new jukebox. Her new acquisition outdid Mr. Alano's phonograph; it inspired the standby boys to gather, jingling their coins for the next song. They now drank at her store, which prospered without any competition. Much later, she opened a hairdressing salon in what used to be Tiya Viring's store. She bought her rival out, hoping that someday her only son would come home alone.

forty

American corned beef sautéed with onions and tomatoes

Mother also hung her heart on the door, like a key as impotent as her wish to leave. Then for all her daily needs and negotiations, she armed herself with spleen, especially against Father's professions of love in the furthest corner of the ceiling, as he gasped over her face and she gasped into the tiny vent. At the other end of the mat, I used to hear them. I wondered why my parents were so desperate for air.

With me gone, perhaps it was Junior who woke up in the middle of the night and listened with dread in his heart. What if it came out twins? Then we'd be eight and there'd be less gruel for each plate. He trusted his ears: if there was too much gasping each night, a baby would come from the armpit. But now that such eventuality was certain anyway, could more gasping mean they'd make it two?

The sleeping arrangement had changed. Junior slept in my old place; he was the eldest now. From where he lay, he heard scraping and shifting. He fumbled the fraying edge of the mat between his thumb and forefinger, in time with the rhythm at the other end. "I love you, Maring, I love you," he heard Father whisper at each gasp. Junior, his fingers suddenly still, waited for Mother to answer. She didn't. Then his fingers were fumbling again in time with Father's grunting, the grunting speeding up, then the gasp, the big one, the last one, and then the sigh, lengthy and drawn out, as if trailing his relief from end to end of the ceiling.

She didn't even sigh.

Father felt proud each time Mother fell pregnant. Many times I saw the slight change in the way he walked. He threw his shoulders back, his chin lifted and his shuffle became a stride, cocky, happy, pelvis slightly forward and feet with a half skip sometimes. And he loved our mother more, bringing her flowers picked from the road or someone's garden. He always looked radiant and his hand or his ear always wandered to her belly twice a day with much affection. While Mother grew more miserable, slow and "overheating," Father glowed, as if he were the one bearing "the promise of joy," for that was how he described it. As if joy were never present but was always in the offing. And nightly he gasped even more.

Junior hadn't been sleeping well since I left. Each time he listened to the predictable breathing at the other end of the mat, he dreaded its consequence, then he felt suddenly hungry, so when all was calm and quiet again, he sneaked downstairs to find something to nibble. Usually there was nothing, so he opened the can where we kept the uncooked rice, took out a pinch, and ground each grain between his teeth, growing more worried by the minute.

Mother said my first brother was born worried. He couldn't sleep each time Father lost his job. Daily he checked the dwindling level of rice in the can, he fretted that he'd never go to high school or that his feet would grow too quickly and we'd have to buy a new pair of shoes for school, which was of course impossible, plus so many other worries besides. Mother said he had a deep crease on his brow when the mid-wife handed him to her.

Tonight he worried about the possibility of twins and he grew hungrier than on those other nights, and it was hotter and he felt angry, though he didn't know why. He curled himself, knees touching chin, trying to press down the noises in his gut, but it wouldn't behave, as if his intestines were having a long-running argument. When Father began to snore, he crept downstairs and did his usual ritual with the pinch of rice, but it left him even hungrier, so he tiptoed to the cupboard where he had seen Father leave the brown paper package that afternoon.

This was a story that he would tell me years later in his weary letters, which always asked whether I could send the family "a little bit of help."

The brown parcel was Target corned beef, all-American. Mother said it was an extravagant, stupid whim.

"How could you, Gable? Every cent of your daughter's hard-earned labor is not for you to splurge on this stupidity!"

"But it was a bargain, very cheap, two for the price of one, and I thought—I thought, for once, our kids can taste something from America."

"So your taste has gone ambitious? Because your daughter is slaving away?"

"Ay, Maring, just a little pleasure."

The little pleasure was bought from an underground warehouse, managed by Mr. Ching but rumored to be the mayor's. The warehouse was stacked with foreign aid; the victims of the eruption had been taken care of earlier. They had received cheap local sardines and small packets of rice, which were distributed by the mayor's bodyguards with a promotional leaflet for the next election. The imported goods had been exchanged with local ones. "As if poor people don't know how to eat imported," Father had thought to himself, so he made sure he brought home his share of the foreign aid.

"For the kids, Maring, don't you understand?" he said. "Just a little pleasure."

"You and your little pleasure—look where it got us," and she started hitting her belly.

"Don't, Maring, please," Father said, gathering her from behind in an embrace that pinned her arms down. "Not this way, not to our promise of joy."

"Whose joy, Gable? Whose promise? And when did you ever keep your promises? Ay, how I hate the lot of you!" she screamed, and freed herself, retreating to the ceiling.

Of course, my father's response was eaten by the devil. Silently, he set the corned beef down, still two cans at that time, and avoided his children's eyes. Their little spines were pinned to the wall, pushed there by Mother's fury. Junior grew worried, then hungry, then surly. He was convinced this turn of events was all my fault, or the fault of my hard-earned labor, my "getting rich." I found out that the twenty pesos that I had laid out on our table soon became the object of my siblings' speculation and hope. So much money! Nining will feed us for the rest of our lives. But Junior resented this: I had left him behind, I had become a grown-up.

He took the can of Target out of the bag, still grinding a grain of rice in his mouth.

How could meat melt on the tongue like this! Father prepared it for dinner while Junior and his siblings watched. This would be their first American meal. All gasped when Father opened it easily with a key that he hooked to the side of the can and rolled round and round—it was magic! They had never seen anything like it before. Then another gasp when the meat came out, not as a rough slab but beautifully molded and proud-looking. Father said it could also be eaten raw, but that it's better like this: sautéed with one onion and one tomato. His cooking flavored the whole house, even the ceiling. They thought Mother would come rushing down to marvel at the new dish but she skipped dinner that night.

It could also be eaten raw, Junior remembered, and of course the key sat on top of the can. In the dark like this, it will be just like magic. He would open it only a little bit and dig out some of the meat with a fork, then he would restore it to its old shape and return it to its brown paper parcel. Mother wouldn't find out, because it was Father who'd cook it anyway.

The next day, an army of ants was discovered trailing across the floor, up to the wall and into the cupboard. Mother followed the trail easily. That was the story of how my brother earned the welts on his back.

forty-one

Escabeche: sweet and sour

Deep sea bream, its head almost the size of his plate. The fish eye had fixed on him an inquiring stare: What brings you here, Ralph McKenna? It was impossible to return the stare. He felt queasy in the stomach, but he tried to smile his crooked smile. "Well, thank you, folks. Very kind of you to give me the best part."

"Try the jaw first, it's the fleshiest," Mrs. Adela Valenzuela advised before she made a little mound of rice, a mouthful, with her fingers.

"And the eyes, very creamy—you have to suck it...uhmmm," her husband added, winking at him.

The queasiness threatened to rise to Ralph's throat. He attempted his usual laughter, but it came out flat. "I'm sure, I'm sure—but this is too much for me. How about you, VV, would you like to share?"

But VV was barely eating, keeping her eyes to her plate. "Huh? Ah, no, thanks." The yellow housedress accentuated her loss of color.

"And you, Nining, our little cook—perhaps you should do the honors instead."

Back home, we loved fish head. Mother could do wonderful things with it. I weighed Ralph's tempting offer, but felt the eyes of my employers on me, so I graciously demurred.

"She's a very good cook." Mrs. Valenzuela patted my hand across the table.

I could see that Ralph's face was competing with the color of his hair again, and there were splotches under his arms, but bravely he forked a morsel from the jaw and brought it to his mouth, while trying to catch my señorita's eyes. I had been watching him since that fateful day when his hand got stained with the *limonsito* berry. I wondered whether my employers noticed at all that it was not the fish and its knowing stare that was causing him extreme discomfort but my ghost of a mistress at the end of the table. He forced himself to swallow, while checking for her approval from the corner of his eyes. "Very nice, yes, thank you," then took a large gulp of the Coca-Cola at his side.

He didn't like my fish *escabeche*? Perhaps he preferred a *peccadillo*—I remembered my employers talking about him weeks before he arrived.

Dr. Valenzuela was laughing now. "Turn on the fan, Nining, it's so hot tonight. Hey, that wasn't too bad, Ralph, was it? Just wondering whether you could eat like a Filipino. Tit for tat. Remember, I could barely swallow the half-cooked rice salad you forced on me at your mum's—rice in a salad, Adela, my God!"

"Andy!" his wife scolded. "What a terrible host you are."

Ralph squirmed in his seat, but laughed with his friend

anyway. Of course he remembered the young Filipino exchange student hosted by his family in Oregon. He weathered all the little pranks that Ralph played on him then and ate everything that his mother dished onto his plate, down to the last morsel. Tit for tat indeed. Suddenly Ralph felt about the same age as that young man, but without the spirit for pranks—"his spark," Andy said. VV's haunted look, which presided over the table repartee, made him feel inadequate and tired.

His host clapped him on the shoulder. "I'm such a bad friend, I know. Relax, Ralph—here, give me that head, I know you don't want it."

Ralph tried to smile. In this country, they even ate dog—during the fiesta, the standby boys offered him some *pulutan,* dog stew that goes with the gin, they said. Poor Spot, poor Lassie. Dog and fish heads, and they clunked their spoons, but what lovely people.

"I'm sorry, Ralph, I didn't mean to embarrass you. The other parts of the fish are actually—manageable." The doctor's teasing quelled his little aversions. "And it's good to sweat when you're eating, it means you're enjoying yourself."

"Thanks," Ralph said as I spooned a filet onto his plate.

"Add some more sauce, Nining," Mrs. Valenzuela said, and I did, and Ralph almost relaxed. I could see the flush receding from his cheeks and he began really eating. "Yes, it's very nice, Andy, very tasty in fact."

"I told you so," the doctor said, relinquishing his cutlery. "And best eaten with the fingers. Follow Adela—c'mon, eat natural, be more adventurous, Ralph," he continued, breaking off the jaw and biting into it. "Uhmm, nothing like fresh fish."

Mrs. Valenzuela efficiently gathered a little bit of rice, a little bit of fish, a little bit of the two other vegetable dishes into a ball and put it into her mouth. I could see Ralph was impressed. Even I was impressed. No one ever managed it as neatly as she did.

Finally our guest was getting enthusiastic with the filet in sweet and sour tomato-ginger sauce, with the zing of peppercorns. "*Escabeche* is a Spanish dish, right, VV?"

"Maybe," she answered without his enthusiasm.

Her parents grew quiet for a moment, studying their guest who was glancing at their daughter's wan face, then at her near-empty plate.

I felt I had to save the situation. "I should have cooked your favorite, señorita, the chicken with papayas, but maybe next time."

"It's all right, Nining, you've done very well today," Miss VV murmured, managing something close to a smile.

I smiled back. With me, she always tried her best to be good-humored. I wanted to feel pleased with myself but ended up with the need to confess. I put a lot of effort into this dish for Ralph's sake because he's actually nice, señorita. You know he watched you singing onstage for the whole night, and he watched you break the *limonsito* in your mouth, and he's watching you now, can't you see?

Much as I loved my mistress and worried about her in those days, at that meal my loyalty was swinging towards the

American. His red hair, his cheeks that flushed and grew pale at intervals, his peripheral glances at my mistress, his crooked smile, his colorful shirts (royal blue this time), and now his very adept use of only his fork. I relinquished my spoon discreetly, trying to use my own fork like a shovel on the soupy *escabeche*—ay, how does he do it?

For a while, my mistress's mood stole all conversation in the room. All I could hear was Dr. Valenzuela sucking the fish eyes and the little bones in a manner both impassioned and neat.

Perhaps like falling in love, eating is passion wearing a semblance of decorousness, when delicacy is out of reach because the palate has just been ambushed into helplessness. The American was all thumbs throughout the meal, even if, in all propriety, he did not dare eat with his hands.

Ay, dae lamang kinutsara—and it was not even spooned. This was our exasperated comment on passions or words allowed to run wild and messy. I imagined Father did not mind such a mess, but Mother, grim as ever, might have kept pushing a spoon at him during his own season of feverish side glances, for surely he had his own early days. Like now, when a middle-aged man hung on to his cutlery perhaps to allay an old fever sneaking up on him—and he thought its shelf life was over after a punishing divorce, that he was safe. Then, suddenly, this ambush.

"Would you like Nining to make you something else, VV?" Mrs. Valenzuela broke the silence.

My mistress looked even more pale, wretched. She was

sweating with extreme discomfort, and one hand suddenly rose to her mouth.

"You okay, VV?" her mother asked, feeling her cheek. "Ay, *Dios ko,* cold sweat—now, this fish is fresh, of course—Nining, are you sure?"

Soon I heard it, indelicate and guttural, a gut turned inside out. Señorita VV was retching into her hand. She stood up and left the table in a rush, her mother close to her heels.

forty-two

Cosido: soup of the Immaculate Conception

A hen clucking at dawn is a sign that an unmarried woman is pregnant? Rubbish. A hen clucking at dawn simply meant that, next door, Boy Hapon had begun reading another Mills & Boon romance. Rubbish. How some people regard Mills & Boon perhaps, because it's too earnest, too simple and embarrassingly sentimental and melodramatic. Romance is not like that. But in this sweet crisis, why then the earnestness of our gut and its embarrassing asides, or when the sweetness turns sour, why the melodrama of our runs or constipations?

Mr. Augusto "Gusting" Alano belched into his soup and wept. Thank God, we were in the outskirts of town and there was no other customer in that *turo-turo,* the "point-point," our version of fast food: all dishes precooked, all you had to do was *point*. But it was long past dinner, in fact it was very late, and there was nothing much to point at but the *cosido,* a sour soup, and the fiery remains of Bicol Express. These and boiled rice made the last meal together of the bandleader and his singer, and me, of course. I was the chaperone.

A grown man weeping was scary. It had sounds, as if there were a full orchestration in his chest. I thought of his tragic divas, their quivering voices, and wondered whether they also wept into their soup. Maybe they did or maybe Roy Orbison did, but not like this. Mr. Alano was looking worse for wear. He was sweating copiously, pomade running down his temple and mouth gaping like an open sore; I could see his gold tooth. His hands gripped the bowl before him as if to catch the tears. I swear I heard them fall, one by anguished one, salting the *cosido*.

The *cosido* is a fish soup, thin and a little cloudy, because of the rice-wash base, and rosy if cooked with purple sweet potato leaves. Its main flavor is the little green lemons. There must be enough lemons to give it authority: it must be face-crumpling sour. No doubt the soup before us had more than authority; it had the mandate of heaven. Surely it was only God who could render grown-ups incapacitated in their grief. While Mr. Alano's gaping mouth could not shut itself, my señorita's face was frozen. She did not even bat an eye-lash, or maybe she couldn't, at the shock over her lover's outburst.

It happened too quickly. It was brought on by the remark, "I'm in nursing, I know what to do." Or perhaps the main cul-prit was the talk about the *Concepción Immaculada*, the Immaculate Conception. This was when Mr. Alano's mouth fell open first and his shiny face began to twitch. We all looked shiny, I knew that, what with the humid evening and the chili. But my mistress's sheen was more of a glow; she always sweated gracefully, except when we had that *escabeche*, of course.

"So, Gusting," she began, then breathed deeply before whispering, "what do we do about this *Concepción Immaculada*?"

His mouth fell, his spoon fell. It made a splash on his soup. "You mean—?"

She nodded. He did not say a word after that, he did not even breathe.

"So?" she asked, fumbling with the clasp of her bag. She held it in her hands the whole time, making me think we would leave any moment.

He started to open his mouth, then looked at me; she looked at me too, as if expecting me to add to the table talk that was soon reduced to monosyllables.

"Sure?"

"Yes."

"When?"

Her mouth tightened and she didn't reply, then she lifted her bag from the table. I was sure we were leaving, so I tipped my bowl and began slurping.

"But we can't have that—that *Concepción Immaculada,* even if—" here, he looked at me worriedly, then turned to her again, voice hoarse, "if Saint Joseph loves Mary."

I could see the slight trembling of her lips, the film of sweat above them. I stopped slurping my soup. I stared at her, I stared at him, and wondered why it was upsetting them—the *Concepción Immaculada,* to the right of the church altar, I remembered. The Virgin Mary in blue and white: eyes raised to heaven, a half-smile on her lips, and arms slightly lifted from her sides with palms open in solemn expectation.

"Gusting, I've been trying to tell you."

"This—this is so sudden. Are you sure?"

"You have to choose."

"But I can't."

"Then we'll end it."

"No! No, VV, give me time—I will—"

"You will?"

They'd been trying to speak in whispers with little success. I thought of my parents at night, their whispered altercations before Mother was hushed and Father started grunting as we tried to sleep.

"You will?" VV asked again.

"I wish I could," he sighed, mopping his sweat with the paper napkin.

My mistress stood at this point. I stood up too and found her hand; it was clammy and ice-cold. I got even more scared. I heard her say, "That's all I want to know," in a muffled voice.

"No, wait, I mean it. Saint Joseph will always love Mary—but I'm sorry, I can't, we can't and you know that, but I told you to be careful, and you're in nursing, you should know these things. Oh, I'm sorry, I don't mean—but—but..." This time, the sweaty face was not only twitching, it began to sag, his inarticulate distress pulling it down to his chest.

She stood very still, like a windless tree. Her hand felt stunned in mine. Finally she said, "I wish Saint Joseph were dead."

"VV!"

In my heart, I too cried out her name, fearful for her blasphemy.

"I'll take care of it. I'm in nursing, I know what to do."

His face collapsed, his lips gave way. I heard the drops on the *cosido* as we walked off. No, he won't finish that.

forty-three

Acharra (the art of preserving)

Like any storyteller, I live on speculations, but always aligned with my gustatory desires. So I imagine that while I slurped my soup through visions of the Immaculate Conception, back in the stone house, Maria Corazón Alano shredded and soaked green papayas. She felt the sweat trickle between her breasts and make a little puddle in her navel. She could not even wipe herself; her hands were coated with papaya sap. It was now eleven in the evening, but still suffocatingly humid. Best to keep busy, she thought, rather than lie awake and sweat till the morning.

Gusting had not yet returned. These days, each time he went for a drive in his old Ford, she was not quite sure whether he'd still come home. She never asked questions and she knew he found her silence unbearable. Ay, the art of preserving domestic harmony. She could almost hear the quandaries in his head: should I leave, should I stay, should I tell her, should I keep silent too and keep up this mad double life? Perhaps he wished she would protest, work herself into anger, chastise him or scream, and push him to confess or leave. Then it would be over.

It was over for Corazón, but leaving did not interest her. And the art of preserving was not for his harmony; it was meant for her pleasure alone. Since she began experimenting with contrary tastes in her kitchen, she had developed an odd pleasure register. These days, the chili bite in her sponge cake thrilled her and even the way a bitter nut broke between her teeth when she ate her coconut muffin. There was always that tiny punctuation on the tongue, the left side; she wondered why. Then she'd take another bite, waiting for the sensation to repeat itself—ah, there it is again, still like a surprise even when she knew it would happen, even when she had put it there herself. Once after a second helping, Gusting asked why she was smiling, then complained that the muffin tasted flat and needed more sugar.

Corazón could no longer stand "just sweet" confections. Today she laid her old carving instruments on the kitchen table, then later ignored them, deciding against flowers and frills. She was making a new version of *acharra,* pickled green papayas, which was usually embellished with carrot or radish florets. She started on a carrot first, using an old penknife, and began carving an arrow, then a tail, a wing with a little dent, and finished with what looked like an ear. She popped it into her mouth; it cooled her tongue and she imagined a breeze picking up outside.

This morning, she had prepared the pickling vinegar and, in an afterthought, some *tuba,* a wicked palm wine. Vinegar is the main preservative for savories, sugar for sweets. The *acharra* used both, but it could do with some wickedness. She would get it drunk, she chuckled to herself, letting the imagined breeze tickle her nape.

When in her heart, a wife decides that she's no longer one, not by her husband's decree or imputation, then she becomes playful. Without leaving, she can be single again, a maiden, a girl. The sense of old self can be recovered and preserved, where it had been adulterated or diminished. Maria Corazón felt like Coring again, as her girlfriends and old flames used to call her, with that affectionate lilt in the last syllable. She took a swig of the *tuba* and smiled. She suddenly remembered what the girls, her bridesmaids, had whispered before she walked down the aisle. "Coring, eating too many papayas makes it go limp. Eating onions makes it do otherwise." Then they took their places behind her, giggling in their frilly dresses.

She surveyed the sweet red peppers on the chopping board. She would not make the usual frills out of them, she thought. They would be little stars instead, paired off with green hot ones. Usually no hot pepper or chili was used in the *acharra,* because it was a sweet pickle.

To be old, to be pickled sour: this was not how she wanted to be when she grew up. As a young girl, like her friends she thought she'd be married, with happy children and grandchildren, and a husband forever holding her hand in the movies or in the park. They would be devoted to each other, they would not be able to eat without the other, they would grow old together, they would die almost together, and if they didn't, they would wait for each other in heaven.

Coring chopped the hot green pepper in two—but there are girlhood memories that must be broken, discarded. One cannot be completely a girl again. This filled her with sadness.

Outside she heard the old Ford pull in. She glanced at the clock: it was close to midnight. Someday even this old habit of checking his homecoming would also be discarded. She began shaping a green pepper star.

The kitchen door opened. She heard him hover behind her. The green star was growing its fifth point and her hand burned.

"Coring..."

The old endearment surprised her and how something in her breast fluttered.

"Coring... I won't leave you..."

It was the stray wind opening and closing her heart, but not because of him. It was because of the girl remembered, a memory hers alone, miles apart from this man promising to stay.

forty-four

Hulog-hulog: gingered drop-drop

Love on the rebound is always suspect. Perhaps because, on the rebound, passion may not have the projectile capacity of the first bounce. "Surely it cannot go very far," everyone in our street said so, when they heard that Violeta Valenzuela got engaged to Ralph McKenna—imagine that! The gossip was that VV had broken her heart over the dashing Basilio Profundo, of course, and was now seeking comfort in this Red Cano, this "Red American," as he came to be known.

"Ay, isn't it too quick, though? And with a man old enough to be her father!"

"I think she just wants to become States-side. Or maybe they already had some hanky-panky, *aysus,* you never know with these foreigners."

The card players shuffled their hearts and made conjectures. "A sudden engagement could mean there's something kicking in there already. Can't you see she's so pale these days?" The standby boys played their Beatles songs on Tiya Miling's new jukebox and seethed with envy. "Why an old man?" And the rest of the street pronounced, "It won't last."

What did they know of the true story? It was I who broke my heart.

It was a Saturday afternoon when she invited me to her room and some green mangoes with hot shrimp paste. We munched and sweated together for a while (hot and sour things make you sweat even more in summer), before she said she was sorry she had been difficult lately and to please not breathe a word to anyone about Mr. Alano. I was raring to ask her about their blasphemous altercation over dinner and her stomping away from the town dance and her generous slices of cake during their jam sessions, but I dared not break her affectionate mood as we lay together in her bed, crumpling our faces at the ceiling. The green mangoes were very sour.

"Promise, Nining?"

I nodded, my mouth too full to answer. She didn't have to worry about me, because by that time, I was willing to do anything for her. I was besotted, I wanted to grow up like her.

"You don't have to pay back the five pesos—that was a gift," she said. And she loved me, she loved me. Even in her distraught moments, she always had a kind word for me, even kinder when the twins left and when I told her about the welts on Junior's back. "You're not my maid, but my little friend," she always said when I told her things. "We have secrets together and we must keep them."

"Thanks very much, señorita," I said, relieved that my next pay would not be five pesos less. "And yes, I promise." A lock of her hair had strayed onto my shoulder. I smelled frangipani and felt conscious of my own sweatiness. I could feel the dampness under my arms and on the top of my crown, and the trickle of sweat settling at the corner of my mouth. I licked it.

"You're the only one who understands me in this house," she said, then sat up, tucking her legs under her. "Even if you don't understand—yet."

"No, I don't, señorita, sorry. Especially Mother. She doesn't want me to sleep at home again, not that I want to go home, I'm working for you, or maybe because she doesn't want my siblings disturbed, but I'm good, I think, and I don't make any trouble there and I don't make any trouble here, do I?"

She shook her head. "You think the world is your fault, don't you, Nining?"

I dipped the last sliver of mango into the shrimp paste.

She got up and looked out her window to the banana and guava trees below. There was something about the way she looked out that made me stare. She was blessing each tree with her gaze. "Ay, all those things that we can't see..." Then she turned to face me. I sat up, hopelessly taken by the picture of benevolence. Framed in light like that with her long, wavy tresses and her blue housedress, and the white lace curtains swishing softly at her sides, she looked like the *Concepción Immaculada*.

Why can't Mother look like her?

"You think I'll like America, Nining?"

I felt a twinge in my chest. Why, is she going away? Will I lose my job?

"You like Ralph, don't you?"

I nodded, wanting to hear more, but she only said, "He's visiting today, so go buy some snacks at Nana Dora's. You shouldn't cook again."

I was confused. But she never cared for the American or his visiting—and did she mean I'll never cook again because she's leaving or was she censuring my cooking? A few minutes later, I was laying my worries before Nana Dora's pot. I wanted our chef of snacks to make me understand why there were too many things that I couldn't understand and whether I would when I grew up, but I couldn't tell her everything really. I did not share secrets with Nana Dora.

"Hush, child, don't sour my food with your worries!" she scolded, dropping the little balls of ground sticky rice into the boiling coconut milk as she stirred it with her paddle of a spoon. Then she was impatiently fanning herself again. "*Aysus,* on an afternoon like this, cooking is like taking a peek at hell, haay."

I watched the rice balls sink into the thick, gingery soup with sweet anise. The *hulog-hulog,* the "drop-drop." After a while the balls would float to the surface, much like Basilio Profundo's *palitaw,* his ardent tongues of two months ago. But unlike them, throughout that summer I would keep sinking, as if the pot's bottom were too elusive, so there was little hope to rise, least of all to bounce. My projectile capacity was an un-heard-of thing, until later when I hitched a ride with VV and Ralph who flew to America and kept rising, on the rebound in-deed for both of them, but how so satisfyingly far a destiny.

"For a young thing, you worry too much," Nana Dora grumbled as she bit into a newly risen rice ball. "Nearly done."

I withdrew my cares and kept quiet, waiting to finish my errand. The *hulog-hulog* grew thicker as it simmered, and the hungry queue began to grow behind me. I heard bits of gossip and the tinkle of coins. This time, like all of them, I could easily dig into my pocket and buy. I did not have to plot or angle for a free snack. I was well fed now. So what followed was a little presumptuous of Nana Dora. "Here," she said, handing me the first cup of *hulog-hulog*. "Eat, it's good for you."

My back twitched in an old pain. I remembered Mother saying the same after she bandaged me. "Eat, it's good for you." But what's good for us, really? And when the seventh child arrived, would it be better? The ginger and anise assailed my lungs. Here was enough flavor to ease constricted chests, to make anyone breathe freely again, but my dread and incomprehension were a load too dense and heavy, and obsessed with its own flavor. No dilution or diminution was allowed, even when I handed her back a clean bowl. "Thanks, Nana Dora, I have money, you know."

"No, that bowl was for free, understand?"

Was she putting me back in my old place?

Then she gripped my chin with both hands, forcing me to meet her eyes. I was surprised. Never had she touched me before. But her voice was scolding. "Hoy, Nining, you know the story of Juan and the banana heart?"

I shook my head, handing her the money for a jar of *hulog-hulog*. I could not look away.

She tut-tutted and continued, "Once upon a time, Juan went to a banana grove one night, to catch an *anting-anting*, a charm, with his mouth. Do you believe in charms?"

Again, I shook my head.

She pursed her mouth, obviously displeased, as she spooned out my order. "Never mind, you listen to the lesson of his story now—hoy, are you listening?"

I didn't want any more of her folk aphorisms. She always thought she understood everything and everyone. When she was not prickly, she was preaching. But I dared not argue. That afternoon I took home a very hot jar of floated intentions and the lesson of the banana heart, the charm that I have kept in my pocket ever since:

"Close to midnight, when the heart bows from its stem, wait for its first dew. It will drop like a gem. Catch it with your tongue. When you eat the heart of the matter, you'll never grow hungry again."

forty-five

Pork knuckle with dried banana flowers

Around the table, there was a shift in appetites. While my mistress became a little bit more engaged with her plate, her parents grew listless and grim, but all their stomachs grumbled alike. Mrs. Valenzuela sometimes came to a meal with red eyes and a sniffle, and the doctor, his lips a thin line, hardly touched his food. Ralph visited every day, eating more earnestly and moving the conversation along, especially with my señorita, who had begun sitting beside him. The doctor sometimes stared at them, sighed and picked at his plate.

The friends seemed to have grown awkward with each other, though Ralph still tried to be charming, always mentioning some detail about American life. Then odd and long silences followed, broken only by the embarrassing asides of the stomach, and I grew teary. The usual appreciative noises about my cooking were now withheld and I thought the cutlery clattered with censure. At each meal, I felt that the end of a friendship and my job was near, but none explained the why and wherefore, most especially the when. Once Mrs. Valenzuela broke into tears when dates were floated around, and excused herself from the table.

At lunch today, there was barely any talk or appetite. My stew did its best to please, steaming its soy vinegar and bay leaf aroma into the air, making it more humid, then grew cold after a while. It was occasionally prodded and picked at, as if the need to eat were only a distasteful afterthought. I could see the American discreetly examining a piece of meat on his plate. He did not flinch when, in my halting English, I explained that it was pork knuckle, but with the toes removed, I assured him. And the long, thin strips were dried banana flowers gouged out of the core of a heart.

The silence that followed was disconcerting. I felt as if my cooking were suddenly under suspicion or reproach, and I had to explain. That I had visited the shriveled hearts in my old haunt this morning and found no banana flowers peeking out of any of them, so I had to look inside. That I was not about to open my mouth under a heart and wait till midnight like Juan, because that was silly and a waste of time, and it was best to get straight to the heart of the matter, then I went on to quote the lesson of Juan's story. I had never given such a long speech at a meal. What followed made my cheeks burn. Ralph took my hand and kissed it, saying, "Thank you, Nenita," then to the rest of the table added, "From the mouth of babes." In his heart he had understood my broken English.

There was no more of the usual after-lunch banter in the lounge room, just the silent mopping of sweaty faces before the doctor and his wife retired to their bedroom, and left Ralph and my mistress alone. From the kitchen, I heard them whispering. I could not quite make out their words, so I edged close to the door and peeked, my hands full of soapsuds.

"You don't have to, Ralph."

"I want to."

"You must be sure."

"I am, Violeta. I want to be with you—and everything that goes with you. That is enough."

I saw her extend a hand and him lean his face towards it, but they did not quite catch each other. It was an awkward gesture, it made them laugh. They pulled back, embarrassed.

"For now, it is enough," she said softly.

I went back to my washing, feeling full in my chest, as if there the banana flowers had bloomed.

Now I should have left it at that and lived with all my incomprehension, for the day at least. But I was set on gouging at hearts and peeking into their cores. After I did the dishes, I sneaked home with a bowl of leftovers without asking my mistress's permission. I decided that appetites could be shifted to another table.

The little scene in the lounge room had left me quite heady and reckless. I will go neighboring. I will lay this bowl of stew on my mother's hands and I don't care what she says, but she will look at me.

Outside I felt as hot and damp as the air. I could see the clouds gathering and dipping low, looking ominous. Ay, to have the heaven open! Our door was black from the residue of ash, in need of a long, good wash. I heard the murmur of voices inside and smelled fried dried fish, even before I walked in. It was half past two, and my family had just started lunch.

There was boiled rice on each plate, not gruel. I took in their faces, sweat-filmed and absorbed, and the fingers as rapt in picking slivers of flesh from the thin, bony fish; I could see there were raw tomatoes too. Everyone looked up as I entered, all eyes on the bowl between my hands. "Ay, what is it, Nining, what is it? Give us a look, quick, quick!" My siblings were all over me and soon my hands were relieved. Father was pleased, and Mother, as always disapproving, asked whether my employers knew I was here with this. Meanwhile five hands had already dipped into this bowl to grab what they could amid a full-blown quarrel.

"That's mine!" Junior said, snatching the biggest pork knuckle from Claro's plate.

"No, mine—I got it first," Claro whined, trying to grab it back.

"Mine, mine," Lydia and Elvis chorused.

"Shut up!" Mother ordered, and Father tried to placate Claro while dipping into the bowl. "I'm sure there's something nicer here for you."

"But I saw it first," Nilo said, trying to grab the piece of meat in turn, but Junior began licking it all over, saying, "You still want it? You still want it?"

Claro began to cry. Nilo chanted, "Greedy, greedy!" The two youngest joined in, banging their hands on the table.

"Stop acting like pigs!" Mother screamed.

Junior giggled. "No, we're not—this is pig," he said under his breath, then bit into the flesh hanging from the knuckle.

"Are you answering back?"

"I didn't say anything, Mama, I'm just eating, as you can see."

"So you're challenging me now, are you, Junior?"

"Maring...Maring..." Father gently began.

"You shut up too!"

Father abandoned his words to the devil and found Nilo a piece of fat from the bowl.

"So, Junior—you think you can challenge me now, is that it?"

But Junior kept gnawing at his pork knuckle with great industry—the fat, the flesh, the gristle—even as Mother repeated her question. Finally she stood up, slamming her fist on the table. *"Lechero ka!"* she cursed, then before we knew it she had slapped my brother. The pork flew from his hand and I saw the red mark spread on his cheek, then he was biting his upper lip and squinting at my mother, who had by now pulled him up by the collar. "You've been acting up for weeks now. What are you trying to prove, you stupid pig?"

We all gasped in horror as Junior pushed her away then dropped on all fours, searching for the meat on the floor. Taken aback by her son's defiance, Mother seemed for a moment unsure, as if her fury had faltered, then she began to kick him, screaming, "Pig, pig, worthless pig!" but Junior did not even cry out. He had found his pork and was eating again, slumped on his chest but one hand still firmly around the knuckle, and he couldn't get up and the kicks wouldn't stop like his eating and I thought my lungs would burst because I was suddenly falling from the sky and the air was rushing past me, I couldn't catch it just as no one could catch me, no one, so my back would break and no one could make it better again so I found myself striding up to her and pushing, just pushing her to the wall and she was looking at me really looking now and I could see the shock in her eyes but I couldn't stop screaming I couldn't stop—

"Nining!"

It was Father. He had caught me from behind, gripping my arms down. "Nining, Nining," he said again and again, his voice growing softer, fading with my name. I could see Mother crouched against the wall, breathing hard and holding her belly, staring at Junior gnawing at the bone. I heard his teeth scrape against the unyielding surface and he could not stop squinting, as if his eyes had conspired with his mouth to break the knuckle open.

I disengaged myself from Father's arms and stood there just looking at her whose eyes were no longer on me. I heard one of my siblings whimper. I retraced my steps to the door without looking back.

forty-six

Shredded heart in vinegar

No one saw me creep back to the house. I curled into bed, pulling the blanket over my head despite the heat. Foolishly I wondered about the boy who could kiss it better, my back, my eyes, kiss them all into forgetting. Especially these—these hands, clumsy and criminal. Walking back with the empty bowl, I had looked out to the red turret and imagined it opened and a Beatles mop flew this way and that.

I listened to my breathing, I counted each rise and fall, sometimes missing the last number thus holding my breath until I remembered, then finally I lost count. I had a siesta.

When I woke up, my dress was drenched in sweat and it was dark. For a while, I thought I was back in our ceiling and if I turned I would bump against Lydia, but there was only the edge of the bed, then suddenly I remembered. Quickly I scrambled up, worried about preparing the snacks—no, dinner now, is it? *Aysus,* how long did I sleep? I rushed out of the room, expecting everyone to be waiting for me with nonstop censure, but the house was so quiet and deserted, as if everyone had vanished into thin air. I tiptoed to the kitchen and turned on the light, then turned it off again, instinctively thinking I should not wake up my employers, for it felt very late. I noted that the kitchen was tidy, everything swept away. I did cook dinner and clean up after, didn't I?

I found myself walking through the kitchen door, out into the open, trying to get some air. I groped my way from the backyard to the front garden, for it was very dark, past the hibiscus, looking up and around, but there was no cross or volcano to restore my bearings. After a while, I kept hitting tree trunks, then I heard noises, like something being slashed or hacked, and then something falling, then another and yet another. It went on for a while. I had kept very still, not daring to breathe, then something or someone brushed past me. I shut my eyes tight, even if I could hardly see anything. When it was quiet again, I tried to retrace my steps back into the house, more disoriented now. Everything felt unfamiliar, the ground under me, the air. I began to run, panicking and bumping into shrubs, thickets, more trunks, I kept running with eyes closed. When I felt a hand grab my arm, I yelped.

"What are you doing here?" the hand asked, and dragged me forward. I was too confused to answer or resist. Then I heard a sudden clucking, and a lamp was lit.

A chicken, on the tallest ladder of Mills & Boons, was watching me with one eye.

"What are you doing here?" he asked again. I could hear relief in Boy Hapon's voice. "I could have hit you, you know. I thought it was a prowler."

"Just walking," I said as the chicken shut its eye again.

"At this hour?"

"I'm sorry."

"You okay?"

"I think—I think I lost my way."

It was a stupid thing to say when I knew our street so well and I had only walked two houses away. "Maybe..." I added, then couldn't speak anymore. Suddenly all the weight of that summer came pouring out of my chest, as if it were monsoon season already and I would flood that little room of chickens and romances. I could not stop crying.

We stood there, facing each other, with me threatening to drown all his Mills & Boons while he held both my hands, not quite knowing what to do beyond this. Through my tears, I could see the sweat following the contours of his cheeks, wrinkled till his overgrown ears and up to his temples, and his upturned eyes did not waver from my face. This close, he looked extraordinarily pale and foreign.

For a while all I could hear was my sobbing and his even breathing, then suddenly there was the flapping of wings and a clucking from different corners of the piled-up books, coming together all at once in a sorrowful crow. It made me stop and Boy Hapon released my hands, saying, "Why don't we sit down?"

He offered me the only chair in the house and proceeded to shove several piles of books together to make himself a stool. Then he lit two candles at the end of the room. He had an altar in that corner, the only one without any books. I did not notice this the last time I was in here, but of course I was in such a state then after falling from the mango tree. His altar did not have the usual Child Jesus or Mother Mary though, but a faded picture of a woman stuck against the wall, with hardly any face left. And before it a lone banana heart, its sap still fresh.

"My mother," he said, then sat down on his Mills & Boon stool. "The nuns said she was my mother." Then he picked up a book and turned to the last five pages and began reading aloud.

It was as I had imagined it. The chickens were all awake, heads cocked to one side in that attitude of listening, beady eyes alert and beaks half-opened, ready to footnote the happy ending, for every Mills & Boon romance has a happy ending. And how they crowed, after every paragraph: when the heroine stopped fighting the hero, when the hero stopped being cruel, when she realized that he was not cruel at all, when he understood that the heroine did not hate him, and finally when all their misunderstandings and incomprehension in the previous two hundred pages were resolved in a kiss.

It was as I had imagined it, but not the conclusion of the reading, for the little ritual did not end with the last word on the page. Boy Hapon picked up the banana heart and cut it in two, and the chickens crowed one last time before he went into the kitchen with the halved offering—for that was what it was, he said.

"I read—and cook for my mother." His words were measured, like a reluctant confession.

He had a mother. The whole street was wrong: he did come from someone.

"You think I'm strange—or crazy—like how everyone here does?"

Was this why he invoked the eruption?

"No, I don't think you're like that at all," I heard myself say softly, then I couldn't help myself. I had to ask what she was like.

"You should look at her picture," he said, both hands stretched as if cupping a face. "Just look at her picture."

He sounded so certain about her, I thought, feeling a twinge of envy. "So you cook and read for her?"

"Every night, but now I've nothing in my garden, no flowers to offer, no vegetables to cook. Even the bittermelons shrank after the eruption, but this heart, it would do—it's a flower, it's a vegetable."

What could I say to that? I helped myself to a knife and began peeling the other half of the heart, as he was doing, making sure I saved only the soft core, the one not yet fully seared by the heat. I knew what he had planned for it, from the vinegar and chili on the table, and from the way he was shredding it thinly. We were making an *ensalada,* which wouldn't be much, as there was so little of the heart that was usable now.

"They said she worked for the Japanese—during the war, you know."

The shreds of heart were not all that smooth in my hands. We'll have to boil these for longer, I thought, so they don't hurt the throat when we swallow.

"That's why I look Japanese. That's why they don't like me here."

forty-seven

No food, no cooking

Someone was shaking me awake, calling out my name, Nining, then Nenita, then Nining again, as if the caller were slipping in and out of an endearment. I turned away from the voice, wishing it would slip out of uncertainty, but it became more insistent. Sprawled on my chest, I felt two pinpoints of pain there, as if my heart had grown a twin overnight, perhaps from too many romances in that house, in that dream—for it was a dream, wasn't it?

"Wake up, Nining, wake up!" I felt arms raise me to a sitting position and the voice continued to say, "You have to go home, Nining, now!" Its urgency made me open my eyes and I saw my mistress holding me, and Claro standing at the foot of the bed, looking very pale and catching his breath as though he had run for miles. "It's born, Nining." Then his voice broke.

I was quickly out the door with Claro gripping my hand as if he would crush it, and saying, "It's not moving, Nining, it's not moving."

My heart pounded as I took in the shocked tableau of my family—we are only six again, I thought, and it was my fault, I pushed her, I killed it. Then everything came alive in a blur—

Señorita VV bundling my mother into their family car and telling us to keep calm because they must take her to the hospital, while my father kept mumbling, "You'll take care here, Nining, won't you, that's a good girl," while my siblings looked on, as far away as possible from the bloody sheets on the floor.

No, we are seven. It is here!

I stood frozen by the door. I couldn't even comfort my siblings, huddled like a flock of petrified birds, damp and disheveled. The humidity in the room was oppressive. Outside it was darker than usual and the clouds hung even lower, like pregnant bellies. I took a step forward, still hesitating. I could see the bundle near the sink, a basin of water beside it as though made ready for a bath.

"Father said to clean it." Junior's voice seemed to float in from somewhere else. It woke me up. I found my legs carrying me to the sink while, in my head, I was going through the motions of bathing my siblings when they were babies. Mother showed me how.

"Will she die?"

It is dead, it is dead, it is dead, I answered in my head, then realized whom she meant. "No, Lydia," I said, then asked myself the same question silently. The answer, also silent, accused me: You wished her dead yesterday. "She'll be okay," I said, pushing back the fear in my heart.

"What do we do?"

Junior still spoke in his strange voice, while shielding the two youngest from the sight of the sheets, but Lydia was peeking from behind his shoulder. Her voice took on a hysterical pitch as she kept asking whether she would die, while Elvis seemed to have stopped breathing on his brother's chest. Behind them, Claro and Nilo were crouched like Siamese twins, paper-white and sucking their thumbs. Claro was weeping silently, rocking back and forth, his brother helplessly conjoined to his rhythm.

"We will do as Father said," I answered, gingerly lifting the edge of the bloodied towel. I saw a tiny fist, blue and rigid, then a bloodstained shoulder, and thought of a chicken that had lost its wing. It's a girl, it is my sister. I kept on telling myself, we are seven, we are seven, so I could go on, so it would be just like before, washing another newborn as Mother had taught me. I kept unwrapping her. I had never seen anything so tiny and crumpled and blue and old-looking. She was caked with blood and white stuff, and her face seemed to have been squeezed into a knowing anguish: I do not belong here.

In my hands, she did not resist as I laid her in the basin of water, one hand under her back and buttocks, the other under her neck as Mother had showed me. I was keeping her head above the water, I was making sure the soap did not get into her eyes. After a while, I heard my siblings rising from their corner, gathering the sheets, then wiping the floor, restoring order, as though they had picked up my rhythm of normality, of life going on again.

When she was all clean and sweet-smelling, I lifted her from the basin and soon Nilo was handing me a fresh towel. I wiped her as tenderly as I could, as I had done with most of them, then instinctively, I laid her against my shoulder. I couldn't help the rocking movement; I had to check myself to stop.

"We must have a coffin." I heard Junior behind me, hovering. He was cradling his old shoebox. "It was the only white thing I could find," he said.

Claro, still sniffling, said there were no clean sheets, but maybe we could use this. He was holding out a white, lacy bundle. "Because it's the prettiest thing in the house," he explained to counter my alarm. It was Mother's wedding dress.

"Here—she will sleep here," Nilo said, patting the center of the dining table, and Claro responded accordingly, spreading the wedding dress there, and Junior laid the box on it, right on the waistline. "And this, her blanket," he said, handing me a white handkerchief, Father's special one.

After a while the two little ones edged themselves towards the table. Lydia was calmer now and Elvis was breathing again. "Look," he gurgled, "look!" pointing at our youngest sister in the box.

"Candles," I said, remembering. "We need candles." Suddenly an altar and a picture with barely a face rose before my eyes—that dream? Such things only happened in dreams, but I was already telling my siblings, "And flowers or vegetables, any offering." Of course I was there, he was there, and the chickens crowed and the heart was shredded, and he told me he came from someone after all. "I'll be back," I said, heading for the door.

I don't think there was any food or cooking that intruded into that moment. Everything about it was raw but without hunger. It was way past noon, but our stomachs had forgotten about themselves. All were gathered around the table not for a meal, but to watch over the white shoebox. I left them, speaking in hushed voices, and found some candles next door. I remember how disappointed I was to find not a single bloom in the hibiscus hedge on my way back, so I proceeded to my old haunt. To pluck my own heart, just like Boy Hapon, no matter how shriveled. A flower and a vegetable for the seventh child.

It was more than grey outside; the sky was almost black and the clouds dipped so low, as if to reach the banana trees just to make sure, just like me, for I couldn't believe my eyes. From each tree hung the curved bough, but heart-less. I checked again, going from tree to tree, but all the hearts were gone, hacked from the bough, harvested. I could not stop gaping until a cloud sizzled with a flash of light, then a clap of thunder—on my upturned cheek, I felt the first drop of rain.

forty-eight

Just water

Agua de Mayo. The first rain of May, after a hot summer, has magical powers. We made sure to catch as much of it as possible with our bodies and in pails and basins, to be stored for healing and for blessing things. When I returned, soaked to the skin, my siblings were already in the street, bathing under the rain and being duly blessed, after having lined up outside all possible containers in the house. To my horror, Junior was carrying the newborn wrapped in Mother's wedding dress, trailing on the asphalt. He was standing still, arms outstretched as if his sister were a precious receptacle that must catch all of heaven's blessing.

I began to scold him, just as Mother would have done, and usher everyone into the house, but no one was listening. I finally kept quiet and stood there with my candles as dripping wet as myself, just watching them. Their bodies trickled with grey grime, for it was not just rain falling from the sky but all the debris of the eruption that had hung in the air for weeks: heaven was flushing itself. The wedding dress was no longer white.

The rain fell in torrents, hitting our bodies, sending us

flinching. Deep puddles rose around our feet and our scalps felt like they were being hammered. "Ay, Nining, rain, rain!" Nilo shouted through the din, jumping up and down, and Lydia and Elvis followed suit, while Claro checked his haul, pouring the grimy water out and setting up the containers again for when the cleaner drops began.

The whole neighborhood was busy catching this outburst of heaven—summer was over. Pails, basins, cans and bottles lined our street, and heads and hands were stretched out of windows to catch the water. Grown-ups usually behaved more discreetly in this ritual, but the standby boys were in a frenzy, throwing cans of water at each other, while the Beatles' "Love Me Do" blared from the new jukebox. Next door, Mr. and Mrs. Alano were at separate windows, resigned that blessings were no longer shared. Meanwhile from Boy Hapon's fringe garden came such clucking, squawking, crowing and all the possible chicken sounds that you could imagine. They had finally flown from their Mills & Boon roost, I imagined, and gone outside, not wanting to be left unblessed. I looked across the street, up the red turret. I thought it was slightly open, but I couldn't be sure.

It was just rain, just water. Without sweets or spices or condiments, without our expert or fumbling interventions to make it taste better, without our need to disguise its nature, but how we reveled in each drop. Sadly love is not just water; we do things to it. We dilute it with other daily longings or the wishes for more, or our fears, angers and sorrows, then our pangs and recriminations, our ludicrous inclination towards endings. If only we could leave love alone, like the uncompromising and uncompromised glass of water at our elbow.

But perhaps we are born compromised to hunger, in all its variations, and just water or just rice or fish will never assuage it. Just water is too fluid and with not enough bulk to fill us, and it passes through our bodies too quickly. So we seek for more and we cook, we spice and sweeten up, we make better, but who can blame us? All the houses in our street knew that the meal at the table was never enough, and surely the air outside tasted of something else, unfamiliar, thus perhaps better?

That summer, I understood that Father's love would never be enough for our mother, and my siblings and I could not make up for his lack. Each time one of us was born, she seemed to hunger for more replenishment and desperately so, as if we were depleting her coffers of affection. Had the newborn been alive, it would have emptied it. But thank God, we were only six again, saved from the seventh hunger. Later, after the funeral, while I anguished that I caused my sister's death, a sense of shameful relief sneaked in sometimes, especially when I watched my siblings eat, always arguing as to who got more and that they wanted more.

But under that first burst of monsoon, there was no wish for more. All we wanted was water.

We stayed outside for a good half hour, waiting for cleaner drops. Claro was especially keen on this, checking his row of bottles and cans, even a basin and a pail for the purer blessing; and he was taking occasional sips, worried perhaps that appearance alone did not ensure purity. Nilo and I began helping him, pouring out the grimy water and starting all over again with this hope for "just water."

By now, Junior was squatting before our door, still holding the seventh child, presenting her to the whole street. Earlier I had attempted to take her away from him, but he held her even closer to his chest, as if he were her only kin. Lydia and Elvis tried to catch their brother's attention, but he shrugged them off. They snuggled close to him anyhow, playing with the train of the wedding dress. After a while, even Claro and Nilo joined the tight circle, faces raised expectantly for the clear drops that would take days to finally come.

"Still so grey," Claro despaired.

"It will get better," I said.

"I wonder whether we should store these at all." Nilo was shaking his head at the brimming containers.

"We should go inside," I said, then turned to Junior. "It will get better."

He blinked at me through the rain running over his face. For a moment, I saw a query there, quickly washed off by the downpour. He hesitated at first, then laid our sister in my arms, whispering, "I'm calling her Agualita—little water."

It was our secret. We all promised not to tell on each other to our parents for the rest of our lives. Not about the wedding dress, which we soaked in vinegar and the strongest detergent to make it white again, not about staying too long under the rain, and not about our own Agualita.

forty-nine

Pinuso: becoming a heart

Mother stayed in the hospital for a week and a half, fighting for her life, and we did not even know it. The baby had been dead in her womb for days. We had never seen our father look so grim, his face tight and set. We wondered whether he had found out about our secret and was angry and biding his time to punish us, perhaps when Mother came home. But to hide fear and anguish, the face must of course shut, even to the ones we love. He stopped looking at us closely as he used to; in fact, he hardly looked at us at all. And he refused to take us to the hospital.

We buried the seventh child the following morning after that first downpour, because Father was adamant that we should conclude this birth and death at once. On the wooden cross, he painted Marinella, after mother's Marina. After the funeral, I came home to take care of my siblings, though I still cooked for the Valenzuelas. Señorita VV made sure the meals were enough for two families; she sent all my cooking neighboring next door. She visited us each day, but I could not understand why Ralph came and spoke intently to my father, as if about some very serious business.

It rained every day. When Mother came home, our street was no longer grey, and the guardians of the sky were back in their appointed places. The cross gleamed as if brand-new and the volcano stood calm and still, as if it had never known an inkling of fire. Heaven was how it was before, with patches of blue emerging, but not our street. It seemed to have shrunk. Mr. Alexander Ching had cordoned his "new" property, the size of which surprised everyone, and resumed construction. My friends' house was demolished and lives were erased. Even our old haunt was soon fenced in with chicken wire. Meanwhile Tiya Miling put up a new sign, staking her own claim. So on the day I went to buy some snacks for Mother's homecoming, I felt as though I had strayed to another street.

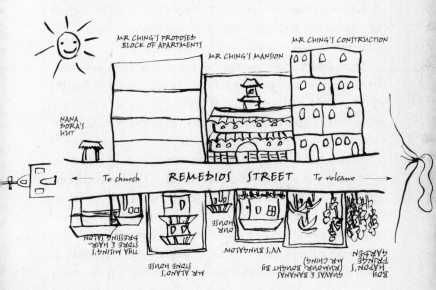

Our street would never be the same again. My friends never plundered those guavas. I never trespassed on that mango branch. I never fell. Tiya Viring never stole the heart of Juanito Guwapito. Tiyo Anding never flew. Imagine our new street, our salvation. Imagine my final rendezvous with Nana Dora's snacks. I walked our street with two points of ache in my chest, where there seemed to have grown twin bumps, one on each side.

Nana Dora did not appear in her usual spot during that first burst of monsoon. Our street missed the delicate melody of her frying and her paddle of a spoon stirring sweetness into the air. I wondered if the downpour had washed away all her sticky rice, her coconuts, her palm sugar, her sweet anise and all the secret condiments that had kept her coming without fail, always on time and with that unwavering intent: to assuage our hunger.

This time I walked towards her hut with a little more confidence, clutching the coins that Father had given me. Surely the world would be all right again at home. He was back at his old job in the Chings' construction and Mother was coming home, saved. But even so, I worried about her return and how I could face her, especially how she would look at me, if she looked at me at all, knowing I had killed it. These were apprehensions that I could not tell my señorita. They sat in my chest; maybe that's why my heart grew a twin, I thought, and both were pushing out, wanting to be acknowledged.

Maybe I could tell Nana Dora instead, ay, there was so much to tell—but we ended up with her doing all the telling.

She left no gaps for me; I could not even begin with my own story about the seventh child. She was confessing tales, which took years for me to understand after that last afternoon in her hut. It was her final transaction with our stomachs.

She rambled over her steaming *pinuso*—literally her "made into a heart," her "becoming a heart." Our final dish. It is ground and sweetened sticky rice and coconut wrapped in a strip of banana leaf shaped into a heart and steamed. It is only a cheap heart at one centavo each. It is small but heavy; it has bulk, it is filling.

"I'm afraid I could never find the balance between my love and anger." The prickliness was gone. There was a quiet sorrow about her as she told me about the Calcium Man and the woman with a womb as barren as soup without water. "You see, Nining, it's the fault of our insides. The heart is not all that far from the stomach, and then there's the spleen just around the corner. So many strange goings-on in there..." She was mumbling, as though talking only to herself. "And you almost think you can perfect eating alone...maybe so. But not forgiving those who abandoned you at the table, for how can you betray that part of you which was betrayed?" Then she said I should go, for the hungry queue had begun. She refused to take my money for the bag of *pinuso*. That was the last time I saw her.

Back home, I unwrapped each little heart for my siblings and my mother. "She's here, she's back," Junior said under his breath. "Father, Ralph and VV brought her home and they talked for a while up there in hushed voices, then Father went back to work. She didn't speak to us yet…she's resting," he explained earnestly.

The twin bumps on my chest throbbed. I worried about how I could face her. I told Junior to take the *pinuso* up to her. He avoided my eyes, saying maybe Claro should do it. How could I know that my brother was also nursing his own guilt—that, for him, the pork knuckle and the stillbirth were the same story, and he would tell it to himself for years? "She'll be okay again, won't she, Nining?"

"She will be—I'm sure," I said. "Don't worry, I'll take this up myself."

A snack and a "getting better" bath in a basin. This was how I had planned her homecoming, so I boiled some water with lime and tamarind leaves, and kept telling myself: I will make amends, I will feed her, I will wash her, I will ask forgiveness, I will be her Nining again.

"Add this to the bath," Claro said, passing me a bottle of *agua de Mayo*.

"It's not pure, but it is the first rain of May," Nilo said, then scolded the two youngest who were trying to climb the stairs. "No, you can't go up yet. Mama must rest."

So I took it up, all our apprehensive love to our mother, in a hot bath and a little heart. I laid it at the foot of the mat, keeping my eyes down. I did not know how to begin.

"You have filled out…"

It was as if someone else had spoken. The voice was depleted, so unlike her.

"I brought food and a bath, Mama."

"Come closer. Let me look at you."

"I didn't mean to, Mama, I'm sorry, I never meant to—"

"Hush…" She was trying to raise herself, so I propped her up with a pillow. She was paler, thinner, like a ghost that could disappear before I had done my duties.

"Maybe we should start with the bath first or else it will get cold. Is that all right with you, Mama?" I asked, dipping the towel into the basin. The scent of lime and tamarind steamed into our lungs.

She closed her eyes, I thought she had fallen asleep.

"Mama?"

It took a while before she spoke again. I dared not start without her permission.

"Would you like to go to America, Nining?"

The towel sank among the lime and tamarind leaves.

"Violeta and Ralph will take you."

My hands sank deeper and stayed there. I thought I heard her sigh.

"You'll be good, won't you, Nining?" She kept her eyes closed, as if she had looked at me enough. "They'll be good to you there, very good… to my firstborn." Then she stretched out an arm to be washed.

EPILOGUE

Sometimes I want to write and tell Mother that I am perhaps the Philippines' first exported domestic helper. She never writes. But during the coldest winters here in Oregon, I linger in the kitchen, the warmest room in the house. Still my kingdom, even if the house is not my own. My new employers say that at forty I should be doing something else, that I'm too bright for the kitchen. Makes me smile. Kitchens need brightness. Here, I'm master of the ritual of appeasement, of making better, and ulti-mately of balance. Here, I know how to keep warm. I fondle the old stones in my head and cast them into the magic pot. Then I add the faithful configurations. Everything will be as it should be. My esophagus its usual length, my heart and spleen in the right place. But sometimes when the flavors get confused, the spleen remembers and I worry that it might grow heavier than my heart, that I will lose the balance between my love and anger. So I write my letter of recrimination. Time and again, I scribble then dispose of it. It embarrasses me, scares me. But maybe I will write it to her sometime, properly and with convic-

tion. Maybe I will even send it. Maybe there's a place for it on the page after all—

   How do I tell you that we were good kids? That there was no need for your sad, furious hands to set us to rights? That I knew how they longed to multiply the meager rice and fish to feed our thousand yearnings? And that they could have done so, easily, had they held my limbs with a little more tenderness? How do I say that I have kissed those hands again and again in my dreams, and now I understand? And it is all right.

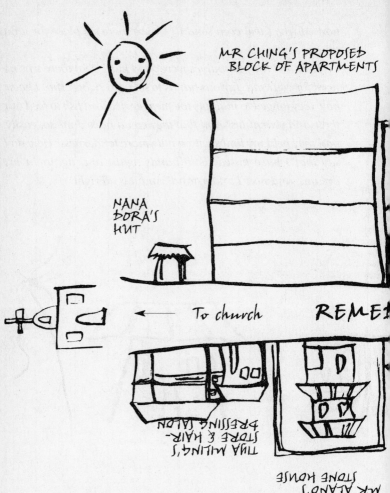

MR CHING'S PROPOSED
BLOCK OF APARTMENTS

NANA
DORA'S
HUT

← To church   REME

TINA MILING'S
STORE & HAIR-
DRESSING SALON

MR ALAND'S
STONE HOUSE

MR CHING'S CONSTRUCTION

CHING'S MANSION

STREET   To volcano →

VV'S BUNGALOW

GUAVAS & BANANAS
(RUMOUR: BOUGHT BY
MR CHING)

BON
HADON'S
FRINGE
GARDEN

Merlinda Bobis was born in Albay, Philippines. The author of poetry, fiction and drama, she has received the Prix Italia, the Steele Rudd Award for the Best Published Collection of Australian Short Stories, the Philippine National Book Award, the Judges Choice Award (Bumbershoot Bookfair, Seattle), the Australian Writers' Guild Award, and most recently the Philippine Balagtas Award, a lifetime achievement award. *Banana Heart Summer* was shortlisted for the Australian Literature Society Gold Medal. Her second novel, *The Solemn Lantern Maker,* will be released in the U.S. in 2009. She lives in New South Wales, Australia.